The Missing Kitten
and other tales

Illustrated by Sophy Williams

Contents

www.hollywebbanimalstories.com

STRIPES PUBLISHING
An imprint of the Little Tiger Group
1 Coda Studios, 189 Munster Road,
London SW6 6AW

A paperback original
First published in Great Britain in 2018

Text copyright © Holly Webb
The Missing Kitten 2013
The Kidnapped Kitten 2014
The Frightened Kitten 2012
Illustrations copyright © Sophy Williams
The Missing Kitten 2013
The Kidnapped Kitten 2014
The Frightened Kitten 2012
Author photograph copyright © Nigel Bird

ISBN: 978-1-84715-950-2

A CIP catalogue record for this book is available
from the British Library.

Printed and bound in the UK.

10 9 8 7 6 5 4 3 2 1

The Missing Kitten

For Emily and the gorgeous Rosie Bumble

Chapter One

Scarlett looked around her new bedroom with delight. It was huge! And as it was up in the roof of the cottage, it was a really interesting shape, all ups and downs. There was a gorgeous window as well, with a curly handle to open it, and a big, wide windowsill she could sit on. Her old bedroom had been tiny, and a very boring squarish sort of shape.

"Good, isn't it?" Jackson, her big brother, put his head round the door. He had the bedroom next to hers, which was basically the other half of the roof space. Mum and Dad had said that their bedrooms used to be the attic.

"I love it," Scarlett said happily. "The window's the best thing! I love seeing all the fields and trees, and look! Cows! Out of my bedroom window!"

Jackson chuckled. "Cows not cars. Now *that* makes a change! Yeah, it's really good. Except everything's a bit far away."

Scarlett nodded slowly. "There *is* a shop in the village," she reminded him.

Jackson made a face. "Yeah, one shop! And a blacksmith. How weird is that?"

"And the school's in the village too," Scarlett added, very quietly. "I wish we didn't have to change schools." That was the thing she was least happy about with their move to the countryside. She was really going to miss her old school, and her friends. Lucy and Ella had said they'd come and stay in the next holidays, but that was a long time away. And meanwhile, she was going to start at a school where she didn't know anyone, and she certainly didn't have any friends.

"It'll be all right," Jackson told her cheerfully, and Scarlett sighed. He wasn't worried. He never was. Jackson was really sporty, and he found it very easy to make friends. And yet he didn't show off, so people just wanted to hang out with him. Scarlett wished she knew how he did it.

"Did you hear that rustling noise?" Jackson pointed up at the ceiling. "I bet there are mice in all that thatch. Remember to tell Mum and Dad about that, Scarlett. You need to start working on them again about a kitten, now that we're here. They said maybe after we'd moved, didn't they?"

Scarlett grinned at him. "I know! I thought I'd maybe give them a day though, before I started asking. Let them get some boxes unpacked first..." She looked up too. "Do you really think there are mice?"

Jackson gazed thoughtfully at the ceiling. "Probably. It sounds like it to me. Unless it's a rat, of course."

"Uuurgh! OK, I'll ask Mum now. No way am I living in a house with a rat!" Scarlett shuddered.

"I'm with you on that," Jackson grinned. "Rats can be pretty big, you know. Bigger than a kitten, anyway." He made a ratty face, pulling his lips back to show big ratty teeth.

"Stop it!" Scarlett cried. "Maybe we can get a grown-up cat then. I don't mind if it isn't a little kitten. I'd just love to have any sort of cat, and they did say maybe we could. You'll help, won't you? You'll ask too?"

Jackson nodded. "Yeah. Although I don't fancy coming down in the morning to find a row of dead mice on the doormat. That's what Sam says his cat does."

Scarlett looked worried. "I think I'd rather have a cat that just scares the mice away…"

Scarlett started her kitten campaign while everyone was sitting down eating lunch. It felt really odd seeing their old kitchen table in a completely different kitchen.

"It's so quiet," Mum said happily, looking out of the open window. "I don't think I've heard a single car since we got here. I love it that we're down at the end of the lane."

"I keep thinking there's something missing," Dad admitted. "But it'll be great once we're used to it. And the air smells amazing."

Jackson sniffed loudly. "That's cowpat, Dad."

Scarlett made a face at him. She didn't want him distracting Mum and Dad – this was a great opportunity to mention a kitten. She took a deep breath. "It's not a bit like Laurence Road, is it?" she said, thinking about their old home. "With all the busy traffic..." She swallowed, and glanced hopefully from Mum to Dad and back again. "You wouldn't worry about a cat getting run over here, would you?"

Dad snorted with laughter and turned to Mum. "You win, Laura. She lasted more than an hour."

Scarlett blinked. "What do you mean?"

Mum reached out an arm and hugged her round the shoulder. "Dad and I were talking about it last night, Scarlett. We wondered how long you'd be able to wait before you asked about a cat. I said that I thought it would be once we'd settled in a bit, and Dad said you'd ask the moment we got here. So I won, and now he has to cook dinner tonight!"

"Simple. Fish and chips," Dad said, taking a huge bite of sandwich.

Mum smiled at him. "You do realize it's a twenty-minute drive to the nearest fish and chip shop now, don't you?"

"You mean you were just waiting for me to ask? So can we have one?" Scarlett said hopefully, eager to get back to talking about kittens.

Mum nodded slowly. "Yes. But we can't go off to an animal shelter tomorrow – we need to do some unpacking, and besides, I haven't a clue where the nearest one is."

"I could find out!" Scarlett said eagerly. "It's just – it would be really nice to have time to get to know the kitten before school starts. We've only got two weeks, and then me and Jackson won't be at home for most of the day."

Dad nodded. "I know, Scarlett, but I

don't think we'll be able to find you a kitten right now. I know it would be lovely to have one while you're still at home. But it won't be a huge problem if you're at school. Mum'll be at work, but I'll be at home working, so the kitten won't be lonely. And your new school's really close. You'll be home in ten minutes."

Scarlett nodded. That was another thing that was different, being able to walk to school. Mum and Dad had even said she and Jackson could walk on their own, if they wanted, as it was all along footpaths.

"I suppose." Scarlett nodded. "So we can really have a cat? You actually mean it? We can look for one?"

"Promise," Dad told her solemnly.

Scarlett beamed at him. She could come home from school and play with her cat. Her own cat! She'd wanted to have one for so long, and now it was going to happen.

"Scarlett! I'm off to the village," Dad yelled up the stairs.

Scarlett shoved an armful of T-shirts into the drawer, and dashed out of her room. "I'm coming!"

She really wanted to walk there. They'd seen the village a couple of times before. The first time was when they came to look at the house. Mum had got her new job at the hospital, and Mum and Dad explained that they would need to move, as it was too far for her to drive every day. Scarlett had really missed her for those few weeks when she'd been leaving early, and not getting back until it was almost time for Scarlett to go to bed. Now they'd moved, the hospital was only half an hour away, in Leaming, the nearest big town to their tiny little village, which was called Leaming Ford. Once they'd made the decision that Mum would take the job, and agreed to buy the cottage, Scarlett and Jackson had gone for a day's visit at their new school, and seen the village again. But Scarlett had been so nervous about the school, she couldn't remember what it was like.

"It's so pretty," she murmured, as they walked along the footpath. "Look at all the flowers. I saw a rabbit last night, Dad, did I tell you?"

"Only about six times! I nearly had a heart attack when you screamed like that. I thought you'd fallen out of the window."

"Sorry! I was excited! I've never seen a rabbit in my garden before!" Scarlett giggled. "Can we go down here? Is it the right way?"

Dad nodded. "Yup, this is the quickest path down to the village, the way you and Jackson will go to school, probably."

Scarlett swallowed nervously. She was still worrying about the school. It was tiny, which was nice, she supposed. There wouldn't be that many people to get to know. But they'd probably all been together since playgroup. They might not want a stranger joining their class at all.

Dad nudged her gently with his elbow. "You had a good time on your visit, didn't you?"

Scarlett looked up at him, surprised.

"It was pretty obvious what you were thinking, sweetheart."

"I suppose. Yes. Everyone was nice. But that was just one morning. I've got to go there every day…"

"It'll be great. You'll be fine, I'm sure you will."

Scarlett nodded. She didn't really want to think about it. "Look – is that the village? I can see houses." She ran on ahead. "And there's the shop, Dad, look."

"I'd better find the list," Dad muttered, searching his pockets. "We definitely need bread. Can you be in charge of finding that for me? Now where on earth did I put it?"

But Scarlett wasn't listening. She had seen something – a noticeboard in the shop window. It was full of advertisements – exercise classes in the church hall, someone offering to make celebration cakes, a nearly new lawnmower for sale...

And a litter of kittens, three black-and-white, one ginger, ready to leave their mother now, free to good homes.

Chapter Two

"Dad! Look!" Scarlett was so excited, she couldn't keep still – she was dancing from foot to foot, pointing madly at the notice.

"What?" Her dad hurried up, peering into the window. "Oh! I can see why you're so excited. 'Ready now', hmmm?" He read the advert through thoughtfully, and then got his phone out.

"Are you going to call them?" Scarlett squeaked excitedly.

"No. I'm going to put the number into my phone, get some bread and milk, and go home and talk it over with your mother. Can you imagine what she'd say if we went out for shopping and came home with a kitten?"

Scarlett sighed. "I suppose you're right. It would be funny though." She giggled. "'Hi, Mum, here's the milk…' And we take a kitten out of the bag!"

"It might have been here a while, this notice," Dad pointed out. "The kittens might all have gone. Don't get your hopes up, OK?"

Scarlett nodded. But as they paid for the shopping, she took a deep breath and smiled at the lady behind the counter. She hated talking to people she didn't know, but this was important. "Excuse me, but you see the notice in the window about the kittens? Has it been up for long – I mean, do you know if they still have any left?"

The lady beamed at her. "After a kitten, are you? Julie Mallins will be pleased. She only put the notice up earlier this week, and I know she's still looking for homes for them all."

"Really?" Scarlett was dancing around again, she just couldn't help it. "Oh Dad, can we go home and talk to Mum about it now, please?"

"All right, all right!" Dad grinned, raising his eyebrows at the lady.

Scarlett ran all the way home – in fact, she went twice as far as Dad did, because he wouldn't run too, so she kept having to turn round and run all the way back to him to tell him to hurry up. When she raced in through the front of the cottage, she was completely out of breath.

"Mum! Mum!" she gasped, running from the living room to the kitchen and back to the bottom of the stairs.

"What's the matter, sweetheart?" Her mum backed out of the understairs cupboard, where she'd been putting coats and wellies away. "Scarlett, you're scarlet!" It was an old family joke.

"Ha ha. Mum, there's someone in the village who's got a litter of kittens they want to give away!"

"Really?"

"There was a notice up in the village shop." Dad came in, holding out his phone. "I've got the number, what do you think?"

Scarlett bit her lip to stop herself shrieking "please, please, please". Her mum was very firm about not whining, and she really didn't want to get on the wrong side of her right now.

"Well, I suppose we could ask to go and look at them…" her mum said, rather doubtfully. "I'm just a bit worried that the house is all upside down right now while we're still unpacking. Wouldn't that be stressful for a kitten?"

Scarlett's face fell. Mum was right. "Maybe we could wait?" she whispered. "Maybe we could just choose a kitten and ask them to keep it for us a bit longer?" She really wanted to have a kitten now, but she didn't want their new pet to start out scared by all the boxes everywhere.

Dad hugged her. "Well, let's see what Julie says – that's the owner," he explained to Mum. "She might not think it's a problem. To be honest, we've done most of the unpacking in the kitchen already. We could keep it in there for the time being – I think you have to keep new kittens in one room to start off with anyway."

Mum nodded. "I'd forgotten that. We used to have a cat when I was little," she told Scarlett, "but it's ever such a long time ago. We'll all have to learn how to look after a cat together."

"What?" Jackson put his head round the kitchen door. "Are we getting one? What's happening?"

"Scarlett found a notice about a litter of kittens needing homes," Dad told him. "We should have known – if there were kittens around, Scarlett was bound to find them! Shall I call this lady then?"

Mum nodded, and Scarlett flung her arms around her. She held her breath and listened as Dad made the phone call.

28

"Hi, is that Julie? We saw your advert about the kittens... Mmm... We wondered if we'd be able to come and see them? Uh-huh. Well, now's great, if that's really OK with you. Fantastic. Kendall's Lane. Oh, off the main road? See you in about ten minutes then."

Scarlett gasped. Ten minutes! Ten minutes till they saw their kitten!

"Here they are."

Julie turned out to be a really sweet lady, who'd adopted Goldie, the kittens' mum, after finding her eating scraps of bread under her bird table, because she was a stray, and so terribly hungry.

"It took weeks to even get her to

come inside," Julie told Scarlett, as she led them through to the kitchen. "But she's settling down now. I think she knew she needed to let someone look after her, so she could have her kittens somewhere nice and warm."

"How old are the kittens?" Scarlett's mum asked as Julie opened the kitchen door.

"Ten weeks – the vet said they should be fine to go to new homes," Scarlett heard Julie say. But she wasn't really concentrating. Instead, she was staring at the basket in the corner, where a beautiful brownish tabby cat was curled up, with four kittens mounded around and on top of her.

"Goodness, she looks tired," Mum murmured.

"Yes, I think she is, poor thing. She's been a really good mum, but she was so thin to start with, apart from her huge tummy full of kittens. I was worried that she wouldn't be able to feed them, but she's done very well. They're all practically weaned now – they love their food!"

Woken by the voices, one of the kittens popped his head up, his big gingery ears twitching with interest.

"Oh, look at him!" Scarlett whispered. "His ears are too big for him!"

Julie nodded. "I know, he's cute, isn't he? He's got massive paws too; I think he's going to be a really big cat."

The kitten gently biffed the brother or sister next to him with the side of his chin, and the rest of the kittens popped up in a line, staring at Scarlett and Jackson.

The other three were black and white, very pretty, without the massive ears. They had enormous whiskers instead – great big white moustaches of them.

"I like the ginger one," Jackson said. "That one's a boy, right?"

Julie nodded. "Yes, and the three black and white ones are all girls."

"I like him too," Scarlett agreed. "Will they let us stroke them? Is that OK?"

"They're usually very friendly. Especially Ginger."

"Oh, is that what he's called?" Scarlett

tried not to sound disappointed. She would have liked to choose a name together for their kitten – Ginger was what all ginger cats were called!

"Oh no. I've tried not to give them names – I'm hoping to find homes for them all, and if I name them I'll just want to keep them. But it's hard not to think of him as Ginger."

The ginger kitten was standing up now, arching his back and stretching as he climbed out of the basket. He looked sideways at Scarlett with his big blue eyes, to check that she was admiring how handsome he was as he stretched. She was watching him eagerly, and she gave a little sigh of delight as he stepped towards her, gently rubbing himself against her arm.

"Oh, he's got boots!" Scarlett looked over at Jackson and her mum and dad. "Look, he's got furry white boots on!"

Mum laughed. "He does look like he has," she agreed. "Those are very cute."

"I know lots of cats have white paws, but I've never seen one where the white goes that far up before." Scarlett stroked the ginger kitten lovingly, and his black and white sisters followed him out of the basket, looking for some attention too. Their mother stared watchfully after them, then seemed to decide that

Scarlett and the others weren't dangerous to her babies. She gave a massive yawn, and curled up for a sleep.

The girl kittens let Scarlett's mum and dad pet them, then they set off chasing after a feathery cat toy, racing round the kitchen and patting it ahead of them with their paws. The ginger kitten watched them, but he didn't join in. Instead he placed a hopeful paw on Scarlett's knee, and she looked back at him, just as hopefully. Did he want to be picked up?

"He's very cuddly," Julie said quietly. "He's a real people cat. Try and put him on your lap."

Scarlett gently wrapped her hands around his gingery middle. Even though he was the biggest of the kittens, he still felt tiny – so light, as though there was nothing to him.

The kitten gave a pleased little squeak, and padded his fat white paws up and down her jeans as though he was testing how comfy she was. Scarlett found herself smoothing her jeans, wanting him to think she was nice to sit on. He padded all the way round in a circle a couple of times, and then wobbled and flopped down, stretching his front paws out, and flexing his claws gently in and out of the denim fabric of her jeans.

"That tickles!" Scarlett giggled, stroking him under his little white chin.

The kitten purred delightedly. That was the best place, the spot he was always itchy. He pointed his chin to the ceiling and purred louder, telling her to keep going.

Jackson joined in, stroking one finger gently down the kitten's back. "His fur's really soft. And look at his paws! They're bright pink underneath!" The kitten was enjoying the stroking so much that he'd collapsed into a happy heap on his side, purring like a steam train.

Scarlett looked down at his paws and laughed – they really were pink. A sort of pinkish-apricot colour, and so soft and smooth-looking.

"They'll probably get a bit darker once he starts going outside," Julie explained. "They've only been indoors so far. He'd need to stay in for a bit longer if you decide to take him." She looked at Scarlett's mum and dad.

Scarlett and Jackson got up, then both turned to look at them too, and their mum laughed. She turned to Julie, and asked hopefully, "I don't suppose you could lend us some cat litter, could you? The shop in the village would have cat food..."

"You mean we can take him now?" Scarlett gasped.

Her mum shrugged. "Why not?"

Chapter Three

"Dad, we're nearly out of Bootle's food. There's only the salmon flavour left, and I don't think he liked that one very much."

Bootle wrapped himself lovingly round Scarlett's legs. He knew quite well what was in those tins, and he didn't see any reason why he shouldn't have a second breakfast.

Calling him Bootle had been Jackson's idea. Scarlett had suggested Boots, but it was like Ginger – a little bit too everyday for such a special cat. Bootle was much better.

Jackson looked up from his huge pile of toast. "We could go to the shop," he said. "I've nearly finished the bread, and there's not a lot for lunch."

"I've got a work call in a few minutes," said Dad. He looked at them thoughtfully. "Though I suppose you guys could go if you like."

"On our own?" Scarlett stared at him.

"Why not? You were going to try it when school started next week, weren't you? If you're careful, and you stick together."

Scarlett shut her eyes for a second at

the mention of school. She was trying not to think about it. "Will you look after Bootle while we're out?" she said seriously.

"Scarlett! You'll only be gone half an hour!" Dad grinned.

"But he's not used to me not being here!" It was true. Scarlett had spent all of her time with Bootle since they'd brought him home, only leaving him at night-time, when he was safely tucked up in his cardboard box, padded out with an old towel, and a hot water bottle to feel like his mother and the other kittens. Just until he got used to them not being next to him.

"I think it would be good for him to see you go out," her dad said gently. "I know you don't want to think about school, Scarlett, but you do go on Monday. Bootle's had a whole week of you around all the time. He needs to learn to be without you."

"But he'll be lonely," Scarlett said worriedly.

"It's only for half an hour," Dad reminded her.

"When we're back at school it won't be!"

"Then he'll have me for company while I'm working. And you know how he loves the computer."

Scarlett smiled. It was true. Bootle was fascinated by Dad's computer. He seemed to love the way the keys went up and down. He would sit watching Dad type for ages, just occasionally putting out a paw to try and join in. Then he would look miffed when Dad told him no. Secretly Scarlett was planning to let him try one day when she was using the laptop she shared with Jackson. She wanted to see what Bootle would write – she knew it would probably be a string of random letters, but she was hoping for a secret message!

"Come on then." Jackson stuffed the last of the toast into his mouth. "Can we get some crisps as well while we're at the shop, Dad?"

"Mmm-hmm. Here." Dad gave Jackson some money. "But I do want change. Be back by half-ten, all right? I don't want to be pacing up and down outside looking for you."

"Are you really worried about school?" Jackson asked Scarlett, as they wandered down the footpath in the direction of the village.

"A bit." Scarlett sighed. "What if nobody talks to me?"

"Why wouldn't they?" Jackson asked, shrugging.

Scarlett shook her head. He was trying to be nice, but he just didn't get it.

"You had loads of friends at your old school," said Jackson. "Why do you think you won't make friends here?"

"It's such a little school," Scarlett tried to explain. "Only one class in each year, and not that many in each class, either. They'll all know each other so well. Like I know Lucy and Ella." She wished she was as confident as Jackson.

He'd already managed to go out for a walk and found a couple of boys playing football. He'd joined in, and then he'd gone back to their house. Scarlett wasn't sure how he did it.

Jackson rolled his eyes. "Come on. We're nearly there."

They went into the shop, and Jackson went to look at football magazines, while Scarlett found the cat food. Then she realized that there were a couple of other girls standing behind her.

"Who's she?" one of them whispered.

"Don't you remember? It's that new girl. The one who came to school for a morning."

"Ohhh! What's she called?"

"Something weird. Amber or something."

Scarlett felt like her stomach was squeezing into a tiny little knot inside her. That was her they were talking about. The one with the weird name. She wanted to scream, "Scarlett!" But she didn't. She grabbed a couple of tins of cat food, and scuttled over to where Jackson was.

School was going to be a disaster. It was so obvious.

Scarlett lay in bed, watching her clock creep closer to seven. She'd been awake for ages, worrying about their first day at school, and now she just wished it would hurry up and be time.

A throaty purr distracted her, and a soft paw patted her chin. Bootle liked her to be paying attention to him, not the clock.

"I'm glad I went downstairs and fetched you before breakfast," Scarlett said, tickling him behind the ears. "I know I look miserable, but you're making me feel a lot better."

Bootle closed his eyes happily, and purred even louder. Scarlett knew all the places he liked to be stroked, and how he particularly liked being on her bed. It was much cosier than his basket.

"I'm really going to miss you today," Scarlett murmured. "I hope you'll be OK. Dad'll look after you." She sighed, a huge sigh that lifted up the duvet round her middle, and Bootle's ears twitched excitedly. He wriggled forward, and peered down under the duvet. It was like a dark little nest, and he wriggled into it, just his tail sticking out, and flicking from side to side.

"What are you doing?" Scarlett giggled. "Silly cat! Oh, Bootle, you're tickling my legs!"

Even the tail had disappeared now. Bootle was a plump little mound travelling around under the duvet. Then he popped out at the other end of the bed, his ginger fur looking all spiky and ruffled up. He shook himself, and ran a paw over his ears.

Scarlett twitched her toes under the duvet, and he stopped washing and pounced on them excitedly, jumping from side to side as she wriggled them about.

"You're awake!" Mum put her head round the door. "Time to get up, Scarlett. Hello, Bootle." She came in and patted him. "Are you worried he'll miss you while you're at school?"

Scarlett nodded, and Mum hugged her. "It'll be fine, sweetheart. Now he's allowed in the garden he'll probably just go out and try and chase butterflies again." She looked at Scarlett. "And you'll be fine too. Honestly. Try not to worry about it."

Scarlett nodded. But she wished she felt as sure as everybody else seemed to.

Bootle sat on the back doorstep, next to his cat flap, staring around the garden. He was confused, and a bit bored. Scarlett had gone somewhere. He'd known that she was going – she had picked him up and made a huge fuss of him before she went, and her voice had been different to normal, as though something was wrong. But he hadn't expected her to be gone this long.

He stalked crossly down the garden, sniffing at the grass, looking for something interesting to do. He sharpened his claws on the trunk of the apple tree, and tried to climb it, but he wasn't all that good at climbing yet, and he only got halfway up before he got worried and jumped down again. Then he had to sit and wash for a while, pretending to himself that he'd never meant to climb it in the first place.

Where was she? Jackson had gone too – he preferred to play with Scarlett, but Jackson was very good at inventing games with sticks, and bits of string to jump at.

Why had they gone away and left him? And when were they coming back?

Chapter Four

"Bootle! Did you miss me?" Scarlett picked him up, and hugged him lovingly, and Bootle rubbed his head against her cheek.

Dad had come to meet them from school, as it was the first day, but tomorrow they were going to walk there and back by themselves.

"Come and have a biscuit," Dad

suggested. "Then you can both tell me what it was like, now there's no one else around." When he'd asked Scarlett at the school gate how her day was, she'd just muttered, "Fine," but he could tell she was only being polite.

"It was all right." Jackson shrugged, munching a chocolate biscuit. "Played football at lunch. The teacher was a bit strict. Shouted at people for talking. But it was fine."

Dad looked over at Scarlett, who sighed. "It was OK. This girl called Izzy got told to look after me, and she was nice. She took me around with her at break and lunchtime. But – well, it was only because she had to."

"She might really like you!" Dad pointed out.

Scarlett ran one of Bootle's huge ears between her fingers, and sighed. "Maybe... It wasn't as bad as it could have been," she admitted. The two girls she'd seen in the shop hadn't said anything else about her weird name, which was what she'd been worrying about. They'd been on the same table as her and Izzy at lunch, and they'd been quite friendly, and asked her where she lived, and if she'd had to catch the bus to school. It turned out that lots of the children did – they came from several different villages, and a school bus went round and picked them all up.

"It's nice we can walk to school," she said to Dad, who was still looking worried about her.

Bootle rubbed himself against her red sweater, leaving gingery hairs all over it, and Scarlett stroked him again. Whatever happened at school, at least she could come home and play with him. She couldn't imagine being without him now.

"You're sure you wouldn't like me to come with you?" Dad asked, for about the fourth time.

"No!" Jackson said. "Honestly, Dad. We're fine. It takes about ten minutes to get to school, and we don't even have to cross a road. Stop fussing."

Bootle was sitting on the bottom step of the stairs, watching disapprovingly as Scarlett and Jackson got ready. They were going again, just like yesterday! Why was he being left behind? He let out a tiny, furious mew, but Scarlett only kissed the top of his head, and went out of the door, leaving him with Dad.

Dad picked Bootle up, and tickled his ears, before rubbing the top of his head. But then he put him back down on the stairs, and headed into the room where his computer was. He was going to be too busy to play, again.

Bootle stalked into the kitchen, and inspected his food bowl, which was empty. He had a little water, and looked at his basket. He didn't really feel like sleeping. And if this was anything like yesterday, Scarlett and Jackson would be gone for hours.

He didn't see why he couldn't go with them. Until yesterday, he'd been with Scarlett almost all the time.

Bootle walked over to the cat flap and sniffed at it, carefully. They hadn't been gone long. Perhaps, if he was quick, he could follow them. Bootle shot out of the cat flap, and dashed into the back garden. Scarlett and Jackson had gone out of the front door, so he hurried around the side of the house, and on to the little patch of front garden. He nosed his way under the blue gate, flattening himself down underneath the wooden panels, and coming out into the lane, next to the car. His whiskers twitched excitedly as he tried to work out which way Scarlett had gone. He could follow her scent, he was sure. He sniffed busily at the grasses, and set off running.

Scarlett and Jackson were halfway to school, walking down the footpath along the side of the big field, which was planted with green wheat – Scarlett hadn't known what it was, but Dad had told her.

"Can you hear a meow?" Scarlett asked suddenly, and Jackson turned round to stare at her.

"Don't be silly. Come on!"

"No, I can. I really can. It's Bootle, I'm sure." Scarlett peered along the track behind them, and laughed. "It is! Look!"

Bootle was running after them, mewing happily, and as Scarlett crouched down to say hello, he clambered up into her lap and sat there,

purring wearily.
He'd had to run
faster than he'd ever
done before to catch
them up.

"What's he doing
here?" Jackson shook
his head. "Yes, you're
very clever, Bootle,"
he admitted, running
one hand down the little ginger kitten's
back. "But now we have to take you
back home, and we're going to be late."

"Oh, do we have to take him back?"
Scarlett said sadly.

Jackson rolled his eyes. "Yes, of
course we do! We can't take a cat to
school, Scarlett!"

"I suppose so."

"And we have to run, because we're going to be late."

Scarlett swallowed anxiously. She didn't want to be late, to have to go in after everyone else, and explain what had happened. They hurried back down the footpath and across the lane before bursting through the front door.

Dad came out of his office, looking worried. "What's happened? Why are you back? I knew I should have gone with you!"

"Don't worry, Dad. It's fine." Scarlett held out her arms, full of purring ginger kitten. "Bootle just followed us. He caught up with us as we were going past the big field – the one with wheat in it. We had to bring him back." She put Bootle into Dad's arms, and he stopped purring and glared at her. He'd gone to find her, and brought her back, and now she was going again!

"Sorry, Bootle. I'd much rather stay with you." Scarlett stroked his head as she went to leave.

"Come on, Scarlett," Jackson yelled from the door.

"You'd better run, sweetheart," Dad said. "I'd drive you, but by the time we've gone all round by the road, it's longer than the short cut. I'll ring the school and explain why you'll be a bit late, don't worry."

"Thanks, Dad," said Scarlett.

When Scarlett and Jackson hurried into the playground, the head, Miss Wilson, was standing at the main door watching out for them.

Scarlett was worried. Luckily, Miss Wilson didn't look cross. She just smiled at them as they raced towards her, and patted Jackson's shoulder. "Don't worry. I used to have a dog that followed me to school. Still, I've never heard of a cat doing it. He must be very fond of you."

Scarlett nodded proudly. She hadn't really thought of it like that.

"I've explained to your teachers, so just slip quietly into your classes, all right?"

"Thanks, Miss Wilson." Scarlett crept, mouse-like, along the corridor. It was all very well to say to slip in quietly, but everyone was still going to turn and stare at her. She eased open the door of her classroom, wincing as it creaked.

But her teacher, Mrs Mason, just smiled at her, and waved her over to her table, and went on pointing out something on the whiteboard.

"I wondered where you were!" Izzy whispered to her. "I thought you might not be coming back!"

"It wasn't that bad yesterday," Scarlett muttered.

"Are you OK?" said Izzy. "Did you oversleep?"

Scarlett shook her head. "No. It sounds really stupid, but I had to take my kitten home. He followed us to school."

"Your kitten did?" Izzy stared at her. "Oh, I didn't know you had a kitten! I've got a cat. He's called Olly. But he's never followed me anywhere! He's far too lazy. What's your kitten called?"

"Bootle." Scarlett smiled proudly. "We've only had him two weeks, and he isn't used to us leaving him. Mrs Mason's giving us a look. I'll tell you more at break, OK?"

Izzy grinned. "You're so lucky having a kitten."

Scarlett nodded, and stared at the whiteboard. Izzy was right, she realized. She really was lucky.

Chapter Five

"I'll keep Bootle inside until after you've gone," Dad said at breakfast the following morning. "If I don't open the cat flap for an hour or so, and I pay him lots of attention, I'm sure he'll stay put."

"I hope so," said Mum anxiously. "We don't want him to wander too far. If he starts going out in the lane and along the footpaths, he could easily get lost." She glanced up at the clock. "I'd better get going. Have a lovely day, all of you. Scarlett, do you want to invite that nice girl from your class round after school one day? What was she called? Izzy? I can call her mum. She could come tomorrow, perhaps."

Dad nodded. "I can pick you all up from school."

Scarlett smiled. Dad had been so pleased when she'd come home the day before and said she'd actually had a good day at school. She would really like Izzy to come over.

"I'll ask her," she agreed, tickling Bootle behind the ears. He was sitting on her lap, hoping for bits of toast. He particularly liked toast with Marmite, so Scarlett made sure she always had

Marmite on at least one piece now. She tore off a little corner, and passed it down to him, watching him crunch it up and lick at his whiskers for crumbs.

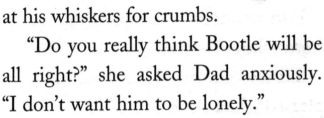

"Do you really think Bootle will be all right?" she asked Dad anxiously. "I don't want him to be lonely."

A cautious paw reached up on to the table, aiming for more toast, and Dad snorted. "He'll be fine. He knows how to look after himself very well. Don't you?" he added, scratching Bootle under his little white chin. "Yes, you're very lovely. Even if you are trying to steal yourself a second breakfast."

Bootle drooped his whiskers, and stared at Dad, his blue eyes round and solemn.

Scarlett giggled. Bootle made it look as though he was starving to death and even Dad was almost convinced. He glanced down at his own plate of toast, and then shook his head firmly.

"That kitten is a shameless liar," he told Scarlett.

Bootle prowled up and down the hallway, his tail twitching crossly. Scarlett had left him behind again, and now his cat flap was closed. He didn't understand what was happening. Why did she have to keep going away?

"Hey! Bootle! Cat crunchies!" Scarlett's dad came out of the kitchen with a foil packet, and Bootle turned round hopefully. He loved those crunchies, especially the fishy-flavoured ones. "Good boy. Yes, Scarlett said some of these might cheer you up."

Bootle laid his ears back as he heard Scarlett's name, and stopped licking the crunchies up out of Dad's hand. Scarlett! Was she about to come back? He looked at Dad hopefully.

"Oh dear. You really do miss her, don't you?" Dad eyed him worriedly. "She'll be back later, Bootle, I promise. Come on, yummy fish things."

Bootle ate the rest of the crunchies, but rather slowly. He liked them, but he would have liked them much more if Scarlett had fed them to him. She had a game where she held them in front of his nose, one at a time, and he stretched up to reach. They didn't taste the same out of Dad's hand.

"Good boy, Bootle." Dad picked him up gently, took him into the office, and put him down on an old armchair. "Why don't you have a sleep?"

Bootle walked round and round the seat of the chair, stamping his paws into the cushions, till eventually he slumped down and stared gloomily at the door. He didn't feel like sleeping, but he couldn't think of anything else to do.

Bootle sat in front of the cat flap, staring at it hopefully, and uttering plaintive little mews. It was still locked. He knew because he'd tried it, over and over, scrabbling at the door with his claws. But it just wouldn't open.

"Do you need to go out?" Dad asked, coming into the kitchen, and looking at him, concerned. He crouched down next to Bootle, who gave his knee a hopeful nudge. "I suppose it can't hurt, it's more than an hour since Jackson and Scarlett left for school." Dad turned the catch on the cat flap and pushed it, showing Bootle that it was open. "Off you go."

Bootle mewed gratefully, and wriggled through the cat flap, trotting purposefully out into the back garden, and straight round to the front of the house, just as he'd done the day before. Next, he was squeezing under the gate, and out into the lane. This time he didn't run as fast. He knew that he'd been shut in the house a long time, and he wouldn't be able to chase Scarlett the way he had the day before.

So he padded down the path, sniffing thoughtfully here and there. It was difficult to follow the traces of Scarlett and Jackson – the cottage smelled of them too, much more than the path, which made it confusing. But he was pretty sure they'd gone this way. Bootle bounded happily along, hoping that they would be in the field again, perhaps sitting down, waiting for him.

But no one was there. Bootle walked up and down the edge of the huge field, staring anxiously into the green stalks. Was Scarlett in there? She might be, but he couldn't smell her, or hear her. He slipped in between two rows of wheat, pushing his way through the green stalks, and mewing.

Then his ears twitched. There was a scuffling noise ahead of him, and a small bird fluttered out of the wheat, making Bootle leap back in surprise. He'd seen birds in the garden, but never up close. He hissed at it crossly, but the bird was already half-hopping, half-flying away. Bootle followed it sadly out of the wheat stalks. He didn't think Scarlett was here.

Glancing around the narrow path at the edge of the field, he tried to remember what Scarlett had been doing when he ran after her yesterday. They had been walking along here, away from him, as though they were making for the hedge at the end of the field.

Determinedly, Bootle padded along, hopping over the ruts and big clumps of grass, and keeping a hopeful eye out for Scarlett. At the corner of the field there was a gap in the hedge, and then a short muddy lane, leading out on to a road with a pavement. Bootle had never really seen a road, and he jumped back, his whiskers bristling, as a car roared past. He had been in a car when he left his mum to come to Scarlett's house, and then when he'd had to go to the vet for his vaccinations, but both times he had been in a basket. From kitten height, the cars going along the road were enormous, and terrifyingly noisy.

He crept into the muddy lane, eyeing the opening out on to the pavement. His ears were laid nervously back, but at the same time Bootle breathed out the faintest little purr. The cars weren't the only noise he could hear. There was shouting, and laughter – the sort of noises Scarlett and Jackson made. He wasn't sure it was them, but it was worth looking. The sounds were coming from very close by. If he was brave enough to go out on to the pavement, close to those cars, he was sure he could find the place.

Bootle dashed out, scurrying along low to the ground, and pressing as far into the hedge as he could go. Every time a car went past – which wasn't very often, thankfully – he buried himself under the prickly, twiggy bits at the bottom of the hedge, and peered out, his blue eyes round and fearful.

The school was only a couple of hundred metres along the main road through the village, and on the same side as the lane. Bootle squirmed under the metal fence at the side of the playground, and scuttled behind a wooden bench, where he sat, curled up as small as he could, and watched the children racing around the tarmac square.

It was very noisy. He had thought Scarlett and Jackson were loud, but there were so many children here. And they were all wearing the same red cardigans and grey skirts, or shorts. He couldn't see Scarlett at all.

He shrank back behind the bench as a loud bell shrilled, and the children streamed back into the building on the far side of the playground. Then his ears pricked up, and he darted forward. That was Scarlett! Racing past him, with another girl. He mewed hopefully at her, but she'd already disappeared inside the white building.

The door was still open.

Bootle padded out into the empty playground, and hurried over to the door. The noise of the children still echoed around the corridor, and he shivered a little. But if he wanted to find Scarlett, this was where he needed to be. He pattered along the chilly concrete floor, peeping in at the doors when he found an open one. The first classroom he looked into was full of children who were smaller than Scarlett, he thought.

A little boy stared at him, and pointed, his eyes widening delightedly. Bootle whisked out of the door as fast as he could. He had a feeling that he wasn't meant to be in here, and he didn't want to be caught before he'd found Scarlett.

The next couple of doors were shut, but then he found one ajar, and looked round it. These children were more the right size. He sidled round the door, and then he saw her, facing away from him, but at the nearest table. The children were all looking away from the door, towards something at the other end of the classroom, so it was easy for Bootle to race across the carpet and hide under the table – right next to Scarlett's feet. He purred quietly to himself. He had done it! He'd found her!

Very gently, he rubbed the side of his head against Scarlett's sock.

Scarlett gave a tiny squeak, and Izzy stared at her. "What's the matter?"

"Something under the table..." Scarlett whispered, her eyes horrified. It was furry. What if it was one of those enormous furry spiders? There were definitely more spiders in the country. She'd found a huge one in the loo at the weekend. Very slowly, she peered under the table, and Izzy looked too.

"A cat!"

"Bootle!"

Mrs Mason looked round sharply, and Izzy and Scarlett tried to look at the board and pretend there wasn't anything under their table.

Bootle purred louder, and patted at

Scarlett's leg with a velvety paw.

"What's he doing here?" Izzy whispered, as soon as Mrs Mason had turned back to the board.

"He must have followed us again." Scarlett was grinning. She couldn't help it. She wasn't quite sure how she was going to sort this out, but she loved it that Bootle wanted to be with her so much that he followed her all the way to school.

Bootle scrambled up on to her lap, and sat there, purring, and nudging at her school cardigan.

Sarah and Millie saw a small ginger head sticking up over the edge of the table, and gasped. Scarlett put a finger to her lips, and stared at them beseechingly. "Don't tell!" she whispered.

Sarah and Millie shook their heads, to say of course they wouldn't. But Mrs Mason had seen them anyway.

"Scarlett, what's going on?" She came over to their table. "Oh, it's a kitten. What's he doing here?"

"He followed me from home," said Scarlett. "I'm sorry, Mrs Mason. He was under the table, I didn't even know he was here till a minute ago." She sighed, a very tiny sigh. She'd hoped to keep Bootle a secret for a bit longer.

Mrs Mason smiled. "Well, he's very sweet, but I'm afraid he can't stay in the classroom. You'd better take him up to the office, and get Mrs Lucy to call home. Is there someone at home who can come and get him?"

Scarlett nodded. "My dad." She stood up, with Bootle snuggled against her, and the rest of the class whispered and aahed admiringly, reaching out to stroke him, as she went out of the classroom.

"You're such a star for finding me!" Scarlett whispered, and Bootle purred.

Chapter Six

"I can't believe you followed me all the way, Bootle!" Scarlett told him again, as she cuddled him in between putting her shoes on for school the next day. "Everybody wanted to know about you. Even people in the year above came to ask who you were – they saw me carrying you up to the office, on their way back from PE." She sighed, and placed him down on the stairs so she could put on her other shoe. "But Miss Wilson made Dad promise he wouldn't let it happen again. He said Miss Wilson was really scary. You're going to hate being shut up for the whole day." She stroked his head, looking at him worriedly. "I suppose in a few days you'll stop wanting to follow me. But I sort of wish you wouldn't. I love it that you're so clever!"

Bootle clambered up a couple of steps – it took a little while, as his legs were still quite short – so that he could rub his chin on to Scarlett's hair while she did up her shoe. He wasn't sure what she was saying, but it was definitely nice. She was fussing over him, and he liked to be fussed over.

Jackson came stomping down the hallway, and Scarlett turned round and dropped a kiss on the top of Bootle's little furry head. "I've got to go. Be good, Bootle!"

Bootle sat on the steps and stared at her crossly as she slipped quickly out of the front door, pulling it closed behind her. She had done it again! How many times did he have to follow after them before she decided it would just be easier to take him with them? He jumped down the stairs in two huge leaps, and made for the cat flap at a run. But it was locked. He scrabbled at it furiously, until Dad came and picked him up.

"Sorry, Bootle. Not happening, little one."

Bootle wriggled out of his arms, and stalked away across the kitchen. He was going to follow Scarlett – somehow.

He would have to get out of the house a different way. Bootle prowled thoughtfully through the different rooms, sniffing hopefully at the front door to see if it might open. He could smell outside, but the door was very firmly shut. And so were all the windows.

But when Scarlett had taken him upstairs to play the day before, her window had been open. Bootle sat at the bottom of the stairs, and gazed upwards doubtfully. They were very big. But he could do it, if he was careful, and slow.

Determinedly, he began to scrabble and haul himself up, stopping every little while for a rest, until at last he heaved himself on to the landing. His legs felt wobbly, but he made himself keep going, on into Scarlett's room, where the door was open just a crack. As soon as he pushed his way around the door, his ears pricked forward excitedly. The window was open! Just as he had remembered it!

Forgetting how tired his legs were, Bootle sprang up on to the bed, sniffing delightedly at the fresh air blowing in.

The windowsill was too far above the

bed for him to reach though. His whiskers drooped a little. How was he going to get up there? He padded up and down the bed and stared at Scarlett's pile of cuddly toys. She liked to tease him with them, walking them up and down the bed for him to pounce on. But why shouldn't he climb up them instead? He put out a cautious paw, testing the back of a fluffy toy cat. It squashed down a little, but it was still a step up, and then on to the back of a huge teddy, and the stuffed leopard … and the windowsill!

Bootle pulled himself up, panting happily as he felt the cool breeze on his whiskers.

Now he only had to get down again on the outside…

"No kitten today?" Sarah asked Scarlett, a little sadly.

Scarlett shook her head. "Miss Wilson made my dad promise he'd keep him in. Poor Bootle. He's going to be so cross."

"He's the cleverest cat I've ever seen," Sarah told her admiringly. "Imagine coming all that way! And he'd never even been to the school before – I don't know how he worked out where to go!"

Scarlett smiled. "It's amazing, isn't it? I think he must have heard us all in the playground."

"You ought to stop in at the shop and buy him a treat on the way home," Izzy suggested. "I've got some money, if you haven't any on you."

Scarlett nodded. "It's OK, I've got some. That's a really good idea." She grinned at Izzy. "You can help me choose." It was so nice having a friend back for tea – it felt like being back at her old school. Izzy's mum had been fine about her walking back with Scarlett – Izzy usually walked back home too. She had a big sister in Jackson's class.

"He might just about speak to us, if we bring him cat treats…"

Bootle scrabbled frantically at the branches of the creeper. It had looked so solid, and easy to climb. But it turned out to be much harder to get down than up. It was also more wobbly, and he didn't like that. The first bit had been easy, just a little jump to that sloping bit of roof, then across the tiles. It was the drop down from the roof that was the problem. His claws were slipping. Bootle gave up trying to cling on, and leaped out, as far away from the wall as he could, hoping that he remembered how to land.

He hit the ground with a jolt, but he was there! In the front garden, right by the gate and the lane. Bootle darted a glance behind him. Then he scrambled under the gate, and set off to find Scarlett, trotting along jauntily. He knew the way now, he didn't have to sniff and search and worry.

He was halfway down the field when it started to rain. A very large drop hit him on the nose, making him shrink back. It was shortly followed by rather a lot of others, and in seconds his fur was plastered flat over his thin ribs. He hid in the hedge, his ears laid back.

He would wait for it to stop, Bootle decided, gazing out disgustedly. He certainly didn't want to go anywhere in that. But it went on, and on, and he needed to find Scarlett. He put his nose out cautiously, and shivered as he felt the drops on his whiskers. It was horrible.

But he couldn't stay here all day…

At last he slunk out from under the hedge, plodding through the wet muddy ruts, and hoping that Scarlett would have something warm and dry to rub him with when he got to the school. He scurried down the pavement, through the puddles, so miserable that he didn't even bother to dart into the hedge to avoid the car going past. The driver of the car didn't see the soaked little kitten, and even if he had, he probably wouldn't have been able to avoid the huge puddle that splashed up over Bootle like a wave. There was so much water that he staggered back, letting out a mew of cold and dismay. Then he flat out ran for the school, racing across the playground towards that lovely, warm, open door.

But it was closed.

It had been wet play, and no one had wanted the rain blowing in. All the doors were closed, every single one – as the soaked, mouse-brown-striped kitten found when he ran frantically all the way round the building.

Remembering the window he had climbed out of at home, Bootle looked up to see if there were any he could get through. There was a bench up against the wall, with a window right above it, and he jumped for the seat, scrabbling desperately until he could heave himself up. Then it was a little hop on to the arm, and then again on to the windowsill. But the window was shut, and everyone was gathered together at the other end of the classroom, looking at something and talking excitedly. They didn't hear him scratching hopefully at the window, and at last he jumped down.

Bootle sat under the bench and mewed miserably, calling for someone to come and let him in. He didn't care if they took him back to the cottage again, as long as he was out of the rain. He would stay at home, and never try to follow anyone, if only he was dry.

No one came. No one heard him over the hammering and splashing of the rain, and the bench was dripping all over him. Bootle crawled out, looking around for another place to shelter. There were trees, over on the edge of the path to the field. Perhaps it would be drier there. He ran through the wet grass, shivering as the stems rubbed along his soaked fur, and shaking water drops off his whiskers. He was so cold. Sitting still under the bench had made him shiver, and now he couldn't stop.

Then something made his ears flick up a little. There was another building. Just a little one, a shed, and he could see that the door was open!

Bootle made one last effort, forcing his shaky paws to race to the shed, and struggle over the step and into the dusty dryness. He was so relieved to be out of the rain that he hardly noticed the sports equipment piled up all over the place – just the heap of old, rather tattered mats that he could curl up on for a rest.

It was while Bootle was fast asleep that the caretaker remembered he hadn't locked up the shed when he'd got out the spare chairs, and came grumpily back through the rain with his keys.

Chapter Seven

"Bootle!" Scarlett called happily, as she opened the front door to let herself and Izzy and Jackson inside. "Bootle, come and see Izzy!"

Dad hurried out of the kitchen, a worried expression on his face. "You didn't see him in the lane then?"

Scarlett stared at him, not understanding. "What?" she asked, with a frown.

"Bootle! He's not out there? I wondered if he'd slipped out somehow. He must have done, I can't find him anywhere." Dad glanced distractedly up and down the hallway, as though he thought Bootle might pop out from behind the wellies.

"You can't find him?" Scarlett stammered. "You mean – he's lost?"

"I'm sorry, Scarlett." Dad ran his fingers through his hair till it stood up on end. "I had a long phone meeting all morning, it finished about an hour ago. Then I went to find Bootle and check that he was all right, but he'd disappeared. I just don't understand how he can have got out!"

"Maybe he didn't?" Izzy suggested

shyly. "He could be shut in somewhere. Olly's always doing that. He climbed into a drawer once and went to sleep, and my mum didn't see him and she shut the drawer. Then she got a real shock because her wardrobe was meowing."

"Maybe…" Dad murmured. But he looked doubtful. "Let's check again."

Scarlett grabbed Izzy's hand and pulled her up the stairs, while Jackson hurried into the living room.

"Bathroom," Scarlett muttered. "Not in here. The airing cupboard, maybe?" She pulled the door open, but no indignant kitten darted out. "Jackson's room…" She peered in, and called, "Bootle! Bootle! He isn't here, Izzy. I'm sure he'd come if he heard me calling. Or he'd meow to tell me where he was."

"He could be asleep. Try the other rooms, just in case."

Scarlett peered into her mum and dad's room, opening the wardrobe, and all the drawers, but there weren't even any gingery hairs. "This is my room," she told Izzy, pushing the last door open. "Bootle!" Scarlett caught her breath. She'd been hoping to find him asleep on her bed, but he wasn't there.

"Your window's open..." Izzy said slowly.

"Oh, but he couldn't get out through that." Scarlett shook her head. "It's really high."

Izzy frowned. "It depends how much he wanted to."

The girls climbed on to the bed so they could look out of the window.

"You see? He could jump on there."
Izzy pointed out the low bit of the roof.
"And there's all that ivy stuff. That's
like a cat ladder."

Scarlett stared at her. "You think he
really could have climbed down that?"

Izzy looked down at the grass, which
was an awfully long way away. "He
might have done."

Dad came in, with Jackson behind.
"He isn't in the house," he said grimly.
"Was that window open, Scarlett?"

"Yes!" Scarlett nodded, her eyes filling
with tears. "I'm really sorry, Dad,
I didn't think Bootle would try
to climb out of it! He can hardly
get up the stairs, and
the windowsill's
really high."

"It isn't your fault." Dad put an arm round her. "I should have checked on him earlier. None of us realized he would be able to climb out of the window." He leaned over to look out. "I think he did, though. Some of that creeper's been torn away."

"Can we go and look for him?" Scarlett asked. "He might have tried to get to school again, and got lost... Oh, Dad, what if he's gone on the road?"

Dad hugged her tighter. "Don't panic, Scarlett. I don't think he would, he's scared of the car noises. Remember how he meowed when we got him out of the car at the vet's? Even though he was safe in his basket he didn't like it when the cars went past. And why would he get mixed up about the way to school, when he made it yesterday?" He let go of Scarlett, and made for the door. "I'm just going to call the school and see if he's turned up there."

Scarlett sank down on her bed, staring up at Izzy. "I can't believe it. Everyone's been telling me today how lucky I am, and how gorgeous Bootle is, and now he's gone. I've only had him a couple of weeks, Izzy! How can I have lost him?"

It was starting to get dark. Bootle scratched at the door with his claws again, but they were starting to hurt. He'd hoped that he could make that little thin strip of light and fresh air bigger, maybe even big enough to squeeze out. But all he'd managed to do was scratch off some of the paint. Miserably, he sank down, mewing faintly. No one seemed to hear him, and it had been quite a while since he'd last heard anyone outside.

Maybe he would have to stay here all night, he thought anxiously. Scarlett wouldn't know where he was. Perhaps she was looking for him? He stood up again quickly, even though his paws felt sore, and meowed as loud as he could. Scarlett would look for him, he was sure of it.

But even though he called and called and called to her, she didn't come, and at last he had to give up. He was worn out with scratching and meowing, and he dragged his sore paws back to the pile of mats. Then he curled up into a tight little ball, and lay there in the gathering darkness, wondering how long it would be before anyone found him.

"We can make some 'lost' posters," Izzy suggested the next morning. "If we ask Mrs Mason nicely, I bet she'll let us use the ICT suite. We could put them up all round the village on the way home."

Scarlett nodded. She should have thought of that the night before. After Izzy had gone home, she and Jackson had searched the house all over again, and then Scarlett had gone to bed, and cried herself to sleep, knowing that her little kitten wasn't curled up in his basket in the kitchen – he was out there in the dark, and she had no idea where.

"We could go round the houses between here and school, and ask if anyone's seen him," she suggested, shivering at the thought of poor Bootle wandering around lost somewhere.

"Ooh, yes," Izzy agreed. "We could get people to check their garages. Don't worry, Scarlett, I can help with that. I know almost everybody in the village, and it's scary if you don't know people."

"That would be great," Scarlett said. She'd do anything if it meant finding Bootle, even if she had to talk to hundreds of grumpy people.

A couple of the Year Six girls came past Scarlett and Izzy on their way in. "Hey, Scarlett! Did you get into trouble with Miss Wilson yesterday?" one of them asked.

Scarlett stared at her in bewilderment. "W-what?" she murmured, suddenly shy.

"When your kitten came back! I thought your brother said Miss Wilson had told your dad off? That he had to keep your kitten at home?"

Scarlett forgot all about being shy. "You mean you saw Bootle? Are you sure it was yesterday?" she asked the older girl eagerly.

"Yeah, definitely..." The older girl – Scarlett was pretty sure she was called Eleanor – frowned. "I saw him looking in the classroom window, but then he ran off. Why? What's the matter?"

"Bootle's lost," Scarlett explained. "Dad had him shut in, but he climbed out of an upstairs window. We think he must have tried to follow us. We weren't sure he had made it to school, but if you saw him, then he was definitely here!"

"You're not mixing up the days?" Izzy asked Eleanor doubtfully.

Eleanor shook her head. "Nope. I'm certain. It was yesterday when it was raining. And your kitten was soaked, Scarlett. His fur was actually dripping. I saw him out of the window; he was in the playground. Before break, I think."

"He must have got out of the window really soon after we left," Scarlett murmured. "Thank you, Eleanor! I have to go and look for him!"

Chapter Eight

There was sunlight coming in from somewhere else, Bootle noticed, as the shed grew slowly lighter that morning. It wasn't just the space around the door. Where there was light, perhaps there was some sort of hole, or another window that might be open, so he could climb through it.

It was up at the top, near the ceiling,

he thought. Very high up. Much higher than Scarlett's window. But then, there were a lot more things to climb in here. Piles of chairs, some benches and more of those mats. He'd just have to find a way to reach it.

Bootle was sure that Scarlett was looking for him – almost sure, anyway. But the shed was all the way across the field from the school, he'd realized, as he lay curled up on the mats. What if Scarlett didn't know about it? He couldn't wait for someone to let him out. He would have to do it for himself.

He stretched out his paws, which felt a little better this morning, though they still ached from all that scrabbling and scratching. Then he padded across the pile of mats, and made a wobbly jump on to an old wooden bench. That was the first step…

"Where do we start?" Izzy asked, as they hurried across the playground.

"I don't know. Maybe we should find Jackson and tell him that those girls saw Bootle," Scarlett suggested, but she couldn't see her brother anywhere, and she wanted to get started searching. "My dad rang up yesterday, remember? And he spoke to Mrs Lucy in the office, and she went and asked in the staff room. No one had seen Bootle. So he wasn't just hanging around school looking for us."

Izzy frowned. "I know I keep going

on about him being shut in somewhere, but…"

Scarlett shook her head. "No, I think you're right! It's the only thing that makes sense. But where?"

Izzy shook her head. "I don't know. Maybe the classroom cupboards? Do you think if we asked Mrs Lucy we could go and look? Oh no! There's the bell."

Scarlett looked anxiously round as everyone began to collect their stuff and head into school. "I can't go into school now! I can't! Bootle's here somewhere, I know he is!"

Izzy patted her shoulder. "It's OK. Look, we'll tell Mrs Mason that Bootle might be here. We have to go in, Scarlett. We'll get in trouble otherwise."

Scarlett almost didn't care, but she supposed Izzy was right. Maybe they could ask the head teacher what to do? She'd said her dog used to follow her to school. She'd understand.

But Miss Wilson was talking to one of the other teachers, and she just waved the girls past when Scarlett tried to hover in the doorway and talk to her.

Mrs Mason was late coming into their class, and when she finally arrived she had her arms full of different coloured PE bibs, and she didn't look as though she wanted to hear about kittens, even though Izzy tried her best.

"Oh dear… Well, I'm sure you can have a look at break," she said distractedly, when the girls tried to explain. "Sit down, please, you two."

Sit down! Scarlett opened her mouth to argue, but Mrs Mason wasn't even looking at her any more.

"Once we've done the register, everyone, I've got some exciting news – we're going to start practising for Sports Day. We've scheduled in a couple of extra PE sessions, and the first one is this morning. So let's just mark everyone in…" She moved names around on the whiteboard. "Where's Keisha? Is she still not well? OK."

"I don't want to do PE," Scarlett whispered frantically. "I have to go and look for Bootle!"

"PE!" Izzy nudged her. "I've just thought! Shut up in a shed, Scarlett, we said he might be!"

"What are you talking about?" Scarlett was biting back tears.

"There's a little shed at the end of the field, where Mr Larkin, the caretaker, keeps stuff that doesn't get used all that much. He was definitely carrying chairs in and out yesterday; I heard him complaining about how wet he'd got."

"So the shed was open?" Scarlett breathed, her eyes widening.

Izzy nodded. "It must have been."

"Now go and get changed, please, everyone," Mrs Mason called. "Then we'll go up to the hall, as it's still a bit too wet on the field."

"I'm not getting changed," Scarlett

said, glaring at Izzy as though she thought her friend might tell her off. "I'm going to find Bootle."

Izzy shrugged. "Uh-huh, and I'm coming with you. Come on."

They hurried out of the classroom, ahead of everyone else, and Izzy grabbed Scarlett's hand. "It's this way. There's a side door, come on." She pulled Scarlett down the corridor, and pushed open a door Scarlett hadn't even known about. "Quick way out to the field."

"Hey, Izzy!" someone called. "We're in the hall, not the field! And you aren't changed!"

But Izzy and Scarlett were already running across the damp grass.

Bootle wobbled on the old chair. He was almost there – he could see the narrow wooden windowsill and the dirty pane of glass. The wind was shaking it, as though it was loose. If he could only get to it, maybe he could push his way out, somehow?

He balanced himself again, teetering on the edge of the chair. He'd scrambled his way up the whole pile, and it had taken so long. If he misjudged his jump to the window, he wasn't sure he'd have the strength to climb up all over again. He was so hungry, and tired, and his paws hurt.

His whiskers flicked and shook as he tried to work out how he could make the jump. It was much further than he'd ever jumped before. And the strip of wood along the window was so very small. But if it meant he could get out... Then he would go back home, and wait there for Scarlett. He would see if he could get back in through the cat flap.

He tensed his muscles to spring, and crouched there, trembling a little, trying to summon up the courage to leap.

Then his ears twitched. He could hear someone! People, talking!

"Bootle! Bootle, are you in there? Is the door locked, Izzy?"

That was Scarlett!

Bootle let out a shrill desperate meow, and forgot to worry about how narrow the ledge was. He just went for it, scrabbling madly with his paws as he almost made it, and then heaving himself up on to the windowsill.

Then he batted his paws against the glass, mewing frantically.

"I can hear him! He is in there, Izzy, you were right!"

"It's locked. I'll go and get Mr Larkin."

Bootle heard feet thudding away, and cried out in panic. They hadn't heard him! They were going!

"It's OK, Bootle. Where are you?"

There were noises outside and Bootle banged his nose against the grubby window, trying to see what was happening.

Scarlett pulled herself up on to the little tiny ledge on the outside of the window. "I can see you! It's really you, Bootle. Oh, I've been so worried. I can't believe you climbed out of a window." She giggled with relief, and sniffed. "And now you're trying to climb out of this one, aren't you, silly kitten."

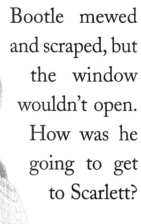

Bootle mewed and scraped, but the window wouldn't open. How was he going to get to Scarlett?

"Oh! Mr Larkin! The keys!" Scarlett's face disappeared from the window, and Bootle wriggled himself round as the door rattled and shook. And then it opened.

With a joyful yowl, he bounded back to the wobbly chair, and took a flying leap to the mats, and then Scarlett was there, hugging him.

Bootle purred and purred, and rubbed his face against hers, and purred louder.

"Izzy! Scarlett! What are you doing out here? Oh! Oh, no, has he been shut in here?" Mrs Mason peered worriedly into the dusty shed.

"All night," Scarlett told her, shivering. "Can I call my dad, Mrs Mason, please? Can I take him home?"

Mrs Mason nodded. "Yes, you'd better take him up to the office again. I hope he doesn't keep doing this, Scarlett."

Scarlett stroked Bootle, who was pressed against her cardigan like he never meant to let go. "Me too."

"Well, he got soaking wet and trapped in a shed, so maybe he'll stay at home now," Izzy suggested.

Scarlett nodded. "He looks like he wants to go home," she agreed, feeling the sharp little points of Bootle's claws hooked into her cardigan. "I promise I won't ever let you get lost again," she whispered to him, feeling his whiskers brush across her cheek. "I'll look after you always."

"I'm really glad my mum said I could come back with you." Izzy sighed happily and blew on her hot chocolate.

Scarlett nodded, stroking Bootle, who was curled up on her lap, with his claws hooked determinedly into her school skirt. He wasn't letting her go. "We might never have worked out where he was if it wasn't for you! He could have been stuck in there for ages – until Mr Larkin had to put the chairs away again."

Bootle purred as Scarlett gently rubbed behind his ears. He was finally starting to feel properly warm again. Scarlett's dad had lit the fire in the living room, and the girls were huddled in front of it – it was raining again, so it had been a wet walk home. They'd splashed through the puddles as fast as they could, anxious to see Bootle again, and check that he was OK.

"Do you want any more hot chocolate, girls?" Dad asked. "Jackson's after another cup."

Scarlett shook her head. "No, thanks."

Izzy smiled at him. "No, that's OK, thanks. It was lovely. It's a pity cats can't have hot drinks, though, Bootle must have been frozen after a night in the shed."

"I've had him on my lap ever since I picked him up," Dad told them. "Apart from when he was wolfing down a massive dinner and breakfast in one. He definitely wanted company, and since he couldn't have you, Scarlett, I was the next best thing."

"I hope he's not going to follow us again tomorrow," Scarlett said, looking down at him anxiously. He didn't look very adventurous at the moment…

Dad shook his head. "No, I'm sure he'll remember being trapped. He won't want that to happen again. But I promise I will make sure every window's closed. I'll even let him play with the computer, Scarlett." He grinned. "I'll find him one of those homework websites, then he won't need to go to school."

Bootle stretched out his paws and stared up at them in surprise as they laughed, and then he huddled himself back into the front of Scarlett's cardigan. It was lovely and warm inside. And dry. He hadn't realized how damp and miserable it could be, following people. For the moment, he was going to stay right here.

The
Kidnapped
Kitten

For Lizzie

Chapter One

"Laura! Laura!" Tia waved, as she rushed down their street on the way home from school.

Her neighbour stood up and waved back. Laura was planting something in her front garden and her beautiful cat, Charlie, was sitting next to her, staring suspiciously at the turned-over earth.

Tia ran up and leaned over the wall,

and her little sister, Christy, followed, panting, "You went too fast for me!"

"Sorry," said Tia, taking her sister's hand. "Laura, guess what?"

Laura smiled. "What? Something good, it sounds like."

Tia nodded. "The best. Mum and Dad say we can have a cat!"

Christy did a twirly dance. "A cat! A cat!" she sang.

"Oh, that's so exciting." Laura beamed at them. "You'll be brilliant cat owners. You were great when you came with your mum to feed Charlie while I was away. He looked quite grumpy when I got back – I don't think I was fussing over him as much as you two were." She looked up in surprise as Charlie suddenly pounced on the pile of earth. "Oh, Charlie! Stop it! You don't want it, you silly cat."

"What is it?" Tia tried to see what Charlie was patting at with his paw.

"A worm. No, don't eat it! Euurrgh!" Laura picked up Charlie and dusted the soil off his paws, and the worm made a quick getaway.

"He eats *worms*?" Christy peered over the wall at Charlie.

Laura grinned. "He eats everything. Especially things that wriggle. Bengals are a bit like that. Really nosy."

"Charlie's a special breed of cat then?" Tia asked thoughtfully. "I've never seen another cat that looks quite like him. He's like a leopard."

"Exactly." Laura nodded and put Charlie on top of the wall so the girls could admire him. He sat down with his tail wrapped around his paws and his nose in the air, posing. "Bengals are bred from leopard cats – little wild cats that live in Asia. Leopard cats are spotty like big leopards. But you can get Bengals with swirly stripes as well."

Tia reached out her hand to Charlie and made kissy noises at him.

Charlie gazed back at her. He had his eyes half-closed, which made him look very snooty, but Tia thought it was actually because he was a bit embarrassed about not being allowed to eat worms.

He eyed her thoughtfully for a few more seconds, then stood up and stepped delicately along the wall to allow her to stroke him.

"You're the nicest cat ever," Tia murmured. She glanced up at Laura. "You know, his fur's almost sparkly when you look at him in the sunshine."

"It's called glitter." Laura nodded. "Lots of Bengal cats have it." She rubbed Charlie's ears. "It's actually because some of his fur is see-through, but it looks like he's covered in gold dust. He's a precious boy."

"Hi, Laura! I hope the girls aren't bothering you." Tia and Christy's mum hurried up.

"No, it's fine. They were just telling me their exciting news." Laura smiled. "If you get a cat, then they can both sit in our front windows and stare at each other!"

Tia giggled, imagining it. Laura's

house was just across the road from theirs, so the two cats really would be able to see each other. Charlie liked to sit on the windowsill and look out. Tia always waved at him on her way past.

Tia ran her hand down Charlie's satiny back again. "Mum! Could we have a cat like Charlie?"

Her mum reached out to scratch Charlie under the chin. "I'm sorry, Tia, but I don't think so. Charlie's beautiful, but he's a pedigree cat. He must have been really expensive." She glanced at Laura, looking a bit embarrassed. "Sorry!"

Laura made a face. "No, don't worry. He *was* expensive. But I'd wanted a Bengal cat for ages. I just loved the way they looked, and I'd read about what funny characters they are. So I saved up for him."

"We'll probably go to the Cats Protection League and see if they have any kittens available," Tia's mum explained to Laura. "Even though you are gorgeous, aren't you?" She made coaxing noises at Charlie, and he did his superior face back again.

"Lucy got Mittens from the Cats Protection League. Lucy's my best friend from school," Tia put in. "She's got a really cute black and white cat, with little white mittens on the fronts of her paws. It's all right, Mittens isn't as beautiful as you," she added to Charlie, who was looking outraged. "Sometimes I think he understands everything we say," she told Laura.

"That's the thing with Bengals," Laura said. "They're very clever. Lots of them have tricks, like opening doors – Charlie can do that. But it means they can be quite difficult to look after. When they get bored, they can be naughty. I wouldn't be able to have Charlie if I didn't work at home. He'd be lonely if I was out all day."

"Cats need company," Tia's mum agreed. "But I only work afternoons, so we should be all right." Tia's mum worked part-time in the office at Tia and Christy's school. "Anyway, we should leave you in peace. Come on, girls."

"Bye, Charlie." Tia gave him one last loving stroke. "See you tomorrow on the way to school!"

"You don't mind that we can't have

a cat like Charlie?" her mum asked, as she unlocked the front door.

Tia turned round and hugged her. "No! I just want a cat of our own, that's all. Maybe a black and white cat, like Lucy's? Will we be able to choose between lots of cats?"

"I'm not sure..." her mum said. "I'll have to call the Cats Protection League. Lucy's mum was telling me about Mittens, and I think she came from a lady who just had a few kittens living in her house. I don't think the Cats Protection League has one big shelter."

"That's probably nicer for the cats," Tia pointed out, as she took off her shoes.

"When's our cat coming?" Christy asked. Christy was only four, and she didn't really understand about the time things took.

"In a little while, I promise," Mum said, and Tia gave a little sigh of happiness. Hopefully they wouldn't have to wait too long...

"Tia! Tia!"

They were on their way to school, and Tia had been daydreaming about what sort of cat they might get. She jumped when Laura shouted after her.

Laura was at her front door, with Charlie weaving himself possessively around her ankles. "Oh, I'm glad I caught you! Is your mum around?"

"She's a bit further up the road, chasing after Christy," Tia explained.

"I don't want to make you late for school, but I really wanted to let you know..."

Tia stared at Laura, not really sure what she was talking about.

"Sorry! I'll start at the beginning. The lady who bred Charlie called me last night – I'd sent her a photo of him, and she was ringing to say thank you. And she mentioned she's got a Bengal kitten for sale!"

"But we can't—" Tia started to say. Mum was right. They really couldn't afford a pedigree cat.

"Oh, I know, but that's the thing. This kitten won't be very expensive. She's got a bent tail. She's still gorgeous, but it's what's called a fault. It means she can't be in a cat show, and no one would want her to have kittens, as they might have bent tails too. So I thought I'd tell you, just in case you want to go and see her. I expect lots of people will be keen to buy her – sometimes people wait ages for a Bengal kitten. I wrote it all down for you." Laura darted back into the house and returned with a scrap of paper. "Here, give this to your mum. It's the breeder's phone number."

Tia looked down at the piece of paper. *Glimmershine Bengals*, it said, *Helen Mason*, and a phone number. But somehow, for Tia, the scribbly writing seemed to say, *Your very own kitten…*

Chapter Two

"Are we sure about getting a Bengal kitten?" Dad asked, looking at the Glimmershine website. Tia had found it for him on his phone, so he could read it while he ate his toast. "It says here about them being *very individual characters*. That sounds like the kind of thing teachers say when they don't want to say *just plain naughty*."

Tia giggled. "Laura said Charlie's a bit like that."

"Mmmm. But he's so friendly with you and Christy," Mum said. "Some cats aren't that keen on children."

"Laura said Bengals can be naughty when they get bored and lonely," Tia added. "But Mum's around in the mornings, and we can play with the kitten after school."

"I suppose so," Dad agreed. "Well, there's no harm going to see this kitten, anyway. What time did she say we should come over?"

"Any time from ten." Mum looked at her watch. "We should probably get going, actually. It's about half an hour away."

Tia jumped up from the table, nearly

tipping over her cereal bowl. Even though it was the weekend, she'd been up since six.

"Slow down," Dad chuckled.

"Sorry..." Tia said. "It's just so exciting!"

The car journey seemed to take far longer than half an hour. Tia was much too jittery to read a book or listen to music. They might actually be getting their kitten! She wriggled delightedly at the thought.

The house they pulled up at looked surprisingly ordinary – apart from a small sign, with a drawing of a cat on it. Somehow Tia had expected something different, although she wasn't quite sure what. She followed her mum and dad up the path, feeling oddly disappointed.

Then Christy clutched at her arm. "Tia, look!" She was pointing at the window on one side of the front door.

The windowsill was lined with kittens. They were all sitting watching the girls walk up the path, their ears pricked up curiously.

"So many of them!" Tia gasped. They seemed to be different ages, too – some of them were much bigger than the others. She tried to count them, but Dad had rung the doorbell, and the kittens clearly heard it. They hurried to jump down from the windowsill – there had to be a chair or something underneath it, as they were all queuing to get down. Except that they didn't queue very nicely, they were all pushing and barging into each other.

Someone had answered the door, but Tia and Christy hardly noticed – they were too busy watching the kittens.

"If you come in, you'll be able to see them even better!" A grey-haired lady looked round the door, smiling.

Tia went pink and hurried in, hauling Christy after her.

The door to the room with the window was closed, and Tia could hear squeaks and bumps from behind it. She stared at it hopefully, while Mum asked about the kitten Laura had mentioned.

The grey-haired lady – Helen, Tia remembered she was called – nodded. "She's a lovely little thing – she'll make a very friendly pet." She beamed at the girls. "So would you like to meet them all, then?"

Tia just nodded, she couldn't even speak. Christy jumped up and down as Helen carefully opened the door.

"I have to open it slowly," she explained. "They get so excited about people visiting, and they *will* stand there just behind the door. I'll catch their paws if I'm not careful." She bent down as the door opened and scooped up a small kitten with golden-brown fur and the most beautiful leopardy spots, who was making a run for it.

"There's always one," she told Tia, "and actually this is the little lady you've come to see."

Tia gasped as the kitten peered down at her. She had enormous round eyes, not green or yellowy, like most cats, but a soft, turquoise blue. Her ears were massive, too, and she had a great long trail of white whiskers.

"Come on in, and we'll shut the door before they all try and escape," Helen said.

The room had been a dining room, Tia realized. It still had the table and chairs, but now there were soft, padded baskets, food bowls and litter trays everywhere.

"It's a kitten room," Christy cried, looking round. "There's so many!"

"Eleven of them," Helen said. "Two litters. The smaller ones are ten weeks old, and the bigger ones are twelve weeks. Ready to go to their new homes."

"Oh..." Tia breathed. "She's old enough to come to us already?" She was still staring at the pretty dappled kitten in Helen's arms. "If she wants to, I mean," she added. Somehow it seemed quite clear that it wasn't only her decision. The blue-green eyes peering over Helen's arm were determined.

Helen nodded. "Why don't you try and stroke her?" she said, lowering her arms a little to make it easier for Tia to reach the kitten.

Very gently, Tia held out her fingers, and the kitten sniffed them thoughtfully. Tia rubbed her hand over the kitten's silky head. "Oh, she's so soft. Like satin."

The kitten let out a mighty purr, a huge noise from something so small, and Tia burst out laughing. The kitten laid back her ears, her eyes getting even huger, and Tia gulped. "I'm sorry, I didn't mean to scare you," she murmured. But the kitten purred again, and Helen slowly held her out to Tia.

"See if she'll let you hold her," she said quietly.

Tia glanced nervously at Mum. But Mum gave an encouraging smile. "She does seem to like you, Tia. You're so good at being gentle."

Tia carefully took the kitten from Helen. "Look at her gorgeous spots," she whispered to Mum.

Dad and Christy were crouched down by the dining table looking at one of the smaller kittens, who was perched on a chair. "She's not quite like Charlie though, is she? Her spots are in rings. Like pawprints!"

"She is lovely," Helen said. "You aren't worried about her tail, then?"

"Oh! I forgot." Tia peered round the little kitten, who was snuggling into the front of her top. It looked pretty much like a normal tail to her, only a little bit bent at the tip. "I love her tail," she said firmly. "It's so dark! Nearly black, and the rest of her looks like – like honeycomb toffee!"

"She does," Mum nodded.

"So … we can really have her?" Tia asked hopefully. She giggled as the kitten hooked tiny claws into her top and started to mountaineer up her shoulder and round her neck until she was standing with her front paws on one shoulder and her back paws on the other, like a furry scarf.

Mum glanced over at Dad, who nodded. "I think she's perfect."

The kitten purred in Tia's ear, as though she agreed.

Tia had hoped they might be able to take the kitten home with them, but Mum and Dad said they needed to get everything ready first. Tia supposed they were right. They didn't even have a cat carrier. So after they'd finally coaxed Christy away from the tiny kittens, they stopped off at the pet shop on the way home.

"Can we buy some toys as well?" Tia asked. "They had lots of toys at Helen's house. I don't want the kitten to be bored at ours."

"What are the chances of that?" Dad laughed. "I don't think her paws are going to touch the floor."

"A couple of toys," Mum agreed. "But

we're not going mad with them, Tia."

"I've got my birthday money from Gran still," Tia pointed out. "I could use that." She stood in front of the cat toys, looking at catnip fish, laser pointers and jingly balls. What should she get? Tia could imagine the kitten loving them all.

She was just trying out a clockwork mouse, when a poster hanging at the end of the aisle caught her eye. It was for the Cats Protection League, asking for donations to feed all the stray cats they took in. Tia looked at it thoughtfully. If her family had adopted a kitten from there, they would have made a donation...

She looked down at her basket and put back the feathery cat dancer and the catnip monkey. She could make a bunch of feathers, and Mum had lots of knitting wool. She would buy the mouse, but that was all. The rest of her money she dropped into the collection box at the till. The bag the lady gave her to take home was very light, but Tia didn't mind.

Chapter Three

The kitten let out a despairing wail. She hated being shut up in the cat carrier. It was too small and it smelled funny, and she seemed to have been in it for ages. But then there was a clicking noise and the door swung open.

The girl was looking in at her now, the one who had stroked her and fussed over her. The kitten nosed forward cautiously. The girl rubbed her ears gently, and the kitten stepped out of the carrier and climbed on to her lap, which was beautifully still after the car ride. Then she peered around worriedly. This wasn't the place she knew, and there seemed to be an awful lot of people and movement and noise.

"She's so quiet," Tia said, as Dad crouched next to her and stroked the kitten.

"She's just not sure what's going on, poor little thing. She'll probably go and explore in a minute."

But the kitten didn't. She didn't go and try out the padded basket they'd bought, or drink from her smart new bowl, or chase after her clockwork mouse. When Tia had to get up and have dinner, the kitten darted off her lap and hid round the side of the cat carrier. She didn't want to go right back in it, but somehow it felt safe. She could have gone with the girl to the table, but there were too many people over there. *Safer to stay by the carrier*, she thought.

"I want her to play with me!" Christy wailed, pushing her plate away. "She sat on Tia for ages! Why won't she play?"

"She will," Mum promised. "She just needs to get used to us, Christy."

"Anyway, we need to think about what to call her," Dad pointed out.

Tia peered at the cat carrier. She could see white whiskers sticking out round the corner of it. The kitten was so pretty, she needed a pretty sort of name – like Rosie, or Coco – except that sounded too much like a poodle.

"What about Milly?" she suggested. "She looks like a Milly, I think."

"Milly…" Mum nodded. "I like it."

After dinner, Tia crouched down by the carrier. She didn't want to scare the kitten, she just wanted to show her that someone was there. The kitten peeped out at her every so often.

Tia had been sitting there for a good twenty minutes when Milly finally edged her way further out from behind the carrier. Tia held her breath. Would she come right out?

"Tia! Are you still there?" Mum asked, coming into the kitchen.

The kitten whisked back behind the carrier with a flick of her tail.

"It's bedtime. Don't worry, Milly will be fine. Dad and I will keep checking on her."

Tia trailed upstairs reluctantly. It felt so mean to leave the little kitten all by herself. She lay in the dark listening to Christy breathing in the bottom bunk, too worried to sleep.

At least she thought she was. She woke suddenly from a dream that she couldn't really remember, except that it hadn't been good. She had been searching for something…

Tia sat up in bed. It was late. Mum and Dad had surely gone to bed – she couldn't hear their voices or the TV.

She could hear something, though. A sad, thin little wail. Yes, there it was again. The kitten!

Tia slid down her bunkbed ladder and padded as quietly as she could out on to the landing and down the stairs. She opened the kitchen door and whispered, "Puss puss... Milly... It's so dark, I'll have to put the light on. Don't be surprised, all right?" She closed the door behind her and clicked on the light, blinking in the sudden glare. She'd expected to see the kitten dart back behind her carrier, or maybe she would be in her basket – but Tia couldn't see her anywhere.

"Milly?" she murmured, turning

slowly in the middle of the room. "Where are you?"

She has to be here, Tia told herself. *I heard her. She can't have got out of the cat flap.* Dad had put the cat flap in, but they had kept it locked – Milly wouldn't be allowed to go out until she'd had all her vaccinations. She was hiding, that was all. *Where would a kitten like to hide?* Tia wondered.

The oilcloth covering the kitchen table moved slightly, as though there was a draught – but all the windows were closed. Tia smiled and crouched down under the table. There, in the dim light under the cloth, a pair of blue-green eyes shone out at her. Milly was sitting on a stool, with the cloth tucked round her like a little tent.

"Hello," Tia whispered.

The kitten stared back at her, and Tia settled herself against the leg of the table. "I'll sit here," she said sleepily. "Just to make sure you're OK."

She was half asleep when she felt little paws padding at her leg, and then Milly scrambled on to her lap and curled herself into a tiny ball.

"Tia! What are you doing under there?" Christy squeaked. "You weren't in your bed – I came to find you!"

Tia blinked. The light was still on and the kitchen seemed very bright. "Is it morning?" she muttered.

"Yes! Did you sleep down here all night?"

"No… I came down in the middle sometime. Owww, I'm all stiff." Tia tried to stretch out her legs without disturbing Milly, who was blinking at her owlishly.

Christy creeped under the table to join them and stroked Milly's back, following the direction of the fur the way Tia had taught her. "I'm so glad she's ours," she said.

"I know," Tia agreed. "I can't wait

to tell Lucy all about her at school tomorrow."

"Oh, hello, you two – you three, I mean." Mum peered under the oilcloth. "Did you come down early to play with her?"

Tia gave Christy a look and nodded. It was better that Mum didn't know she'd been downstairs half the night...

After that first night, Milly settled in quickly. She didn't stay confined to the kitchen for long – she was far too nosy. She missed her old home and all her brothers and sisters, but now she had a whole house to explore. She explored it properly, too – every surface, every shelf, every cupboard. She wasn't big enough to climb the stairs at first, but whenever Tia and Christy were home, they were happy to carry her. And by the time she had been living with Tia's family for a month, she was big enough to scramble up them by herself.

Milly's favourite place was Tia and Christy's room. It was full of toys to chase and boxes to wriggle in and out of. She was also fascinated by the ladder to Tia's top bunk. Tia had carried her up there, but Milly wanted to be able to climb it on her own.

"What are you doing, kitten?" Tia said, laughing as she watched Milly from her desk. She was trying to do her homework, but Milly kept stealing her pencils and burying them under the bed.

Milly put her front paws on the first step – the ladder had flat, wide rungs, and it was easy enough to jump on to one. She managed to jump from the first step to the second. But then she wobbled and slid, and had to make a flying leap down on to Christy's bed instead. Then she went prowling off through the soft toys, pretending that was what she had meant to do all along.

Tia wished she could play with Milly, but she had to finish her homework first.

It wasn't until Christy came upstairs and let out a piercing shriek that Tia realized what Milly had been doing. One of Christy's favourite toys was a feathery owl that Dad had brought back for her from a work trip. It always sat propped up at the side of her bed because it was made up of lots of tiny feathers and it was a bit fragile.

"Owly! She's eaten Owly!" Christy howled.

Milly sat in the middle of the bed, looking rather confused. Christy did burst out crying every so often, she'd got used to that now. But she was being very loud and she was stamping about. Milly spat out a mouthful of the interesting feathers and slunk to the end of the bed, making for Tia.

"Whatever's the matter?" Mum said,

175

rushing in. "Oh my goodness. Christy, I'm sorry, sweetheart."

"He's all eaten and ruined…" Christy sobbed.

"Tia, how on earth could you have let Milly do that?" Mum asked.

"I didn't see! I was doing my homework. Sorry, Christy…" Tia picked Milly up, looking guiltily at her little sister. "Maybe we can glue the feathers back on."

"You shouldn't cuddle her," Christy growled. "She's a bad cat!"

"Oh no, she isn't! She didn't know."

Milly snuggled closer into Tia's school jumper, not liking the angry voices.

"You're scaring her!" Tia said, and Christy wailed again.

"I don't care! She broke Owly!"

"Take that cat downstairs, Tia," Mum snapped. "Honestly, after the pavlova yesterday as well. I never thought a kitten could be so much trouble."

"I wish we had a kitten that didn't eat things!" Christy gulped.

Tia hurried down the stairs with Milly in her arms. "You are silly," she muttered. "I love you climbing about and getting into everything, but the pavlova was a disaster."

Mum had been making a lovely pudding to take to a friend's house, and she'd left it out on the counter while she answered the door. She came back to find a very happy cat, and a lot less whipped cream on top of the pavlova. Mum had had to buy a pudding instead, although Tia was sure it would have been all right if Mum had just moved the raspberries around a bit.

"I think you'd better try and be perfectly behaved for the next few days," she told Milly, as she put her in her basket. "You're definitely not Mum or Christy's favourite cat right now."

"You don't think there's anything I can do about Milly, then?" Tia asked Laura, sipping at her juice. It was the weekend, and she'd popped over to get some advice on Milly's naughty tricks.

Laura shook her head slowly. "Not much. Just make her get down every time you see her somewhere she shouldn't be. A lot of it's simply that she's a kitten. She will get better as she gets older. Charlie used to knock things over all the time, but he doesn't do quite so much climbing now."

Tia sighed. It didn't look like there was an easy answer. "I guess I'm lucky she hasn't really spoiled anything of mine yet. Well, she did eat my sandwiches yesterday while Mum was doing my packed lunch. But that's not the same as Owly. Christy is still really upset. She says we should take Milly back and get a better-behaved cat."

"I suppose the thing to do is make sure anything precious is put away," Laura said. "And shut the doors if there are rooms you don't want her in."

"Mmmm," Tia agreed. "It's just Christy *never* shuts doors."

"Milly might learn to open them anyway. I wouldn't be surprised. Actually, Tia, I'm glad you came over," Laura said, reaching over to a pile of newspapers on one of the kitchen chairs. "I was going to talk to your mum or dad. Do you know if they've seen this?" She folded the newspaper over and showed a headline to Tia – CATNAPPERS STEAL PRECIOUS PETS.

"No!" Tia looked at it in horror. "Why are they stealing them?"

"To sell." Laura was frowning. "It's because pedigree cats are so expensive. The thieves steal them and then sell them for less than you'd pay at a breeder. I'm sure most of the people don't realize the cats are stolen. The thing is, this article particularly mentions Bengals. Because they're so fashionable. And I know that one lady who has one of Charlie's littermates caught someone trying to tempt her cat out of her garden. She doesn't live all that far from here."

Tia jumped up from the table. "I'm really sorry, Laura, but I have to go home. Milly's allowed out of her cat flap now. What if someone's trying to steal her this minute?"

Chapter Four

Laura tried to tell Tia that it was unlikely anyone would try and steal Milly, and she hadn't meant to scare her. She was still letting Charlie go out, but only when she was around to keep an eye on him. "Just to be safe," she explained.

Tia calmed down enough to finish her juice. But she refused a biscuit, and as she hurried back home she couldn't help keeping an eye out for cat thieves. *What would they look like, though?*

Tia went down the side of her house to the back garden. Milly loved it out there. She bounced in and out of the plants, and spied on the bird table. Tia had noticed that only the bravest birds came to it now.

But Milly wasn't sitting underneath the bird table and she didn't come when Tia called, like she usually did. She was nowhere to be seen.

"Milly! Milly!" Tia called anxiously. She ran down the garden to look over the back fence into Mr Jackson's garden. Milly liked it over there. Mr Jackson had a goldfish pond. She had climbed the fence at the side of the garden, too, but the people next door had a spaniel called Max, and he had barked at Milly so loudly that she'd jumped straight down again.

Just as Tia reached the back fence and looked through the trellis on the top, there was a splashing sound and a horrified yowl. Then something bounded across Mr Jackson's garden. A small, bedraggled thing, trailing long streamers of green weed.

"That cat of yours is after my goldfish!" Mr Jackson shouted crossly to Tia. "Little menace!"

Milly jumped on to Mr Jackson's compost bin and then up on to the fence, where Tia reached up and grabbed her. She shuddered at the clammy wet fur – Milly was soaking.

"I'm really sorry!" Tia gasped to the old man. "We'll keep her inside!"

"We'll have to," she murmured to Milly, as she carried her down the garden. "Maybe we'd better lock the catflap, so you can only go out when one of us with you. I know you won't like that much, but I'm not going to let anyone steal you!"

Tia was quite right. Milly was most unimpressed with being shut inside. She always followed Tia and Christy when they went out into the garden.

She would chase the football, and sometimes Tia carried her up on to their climbing frame. Christy had forgiven her for shredding Owly now, and she would dance down the garden trailing bits of string for Milly to pounce on. But sometimes Milly wanted to go outside on her own, too. It wasn't the same watching the birds from the kitchen windowsill.

Often she sat in the front window instead, especially in the afternoon, when she knew that Tia and Christy would soon be home. People sometimes pointed at her, and Milly could tell that they were saying nice things. One blond-haired man seemed to walk past the house quite often, just to see her. He always stopped and looked at her for ages. And at the other cat, the one that lived across the road.

Milly liked to stare at the other cat as well. But he usually pretended not to see her.

"Look, Christy, Milly's watching for us again," Tia pointed to Milly, sitting in the front window, and Milly leaped for the back of the sofa. She would jump from there to the arm, and then on to the floor to meet them at the front door.

"Nice cat!" There was a young man with blond hair walking slowly past their house on the way to his van. He was jingling the keys in his hand, and he smiled at Tia and Christy. "Is she yours? Does she always run and meet you like that?"

Tia smiled back. She loved it when people admired Milly. "Yes," she said proudly.

"She's beautiful. What is she, a Bengal?"

"Yes, she's four months old," Tia said.

The man smiled again and walked over to his blue van, which was parked further up the road.

Mum hurried up behind them. "Who was that you were talking to?" she asked.

"Oh – well, he was asking about Milly," Tia said, frowning. She hadn't really thought about it, but the man was a stranger, of course. "He seemed nice…" she added.

"No, he wasn't," Christy said firmly. "*I* didn't like him."

"Oh, don't be silly, Christy," Tia muttered, as Mum started to tell her off for chatting to people she didn't know.

"You were just coming, Mum. You were almost with us," Tia muttered. But she had a horrible feeling now that Mum and Christy were right. She shouldn't have spoken to him. She sighed. "I suppose we shouldn't tell people Milly's a Bengal, should we? In case someone tries to steal her."

Mum put an arm around her shoulder. "I'm sure that won't happen, Tia. But next time, just say that I'm the person to ask, and come and get me!

Come on, let's get in the house. Milly's probably having a fit by now."

Tia had hoped that Milly would get used to staying inside, but the kitten still took every chance she could to sneak out. And she moved so fast she was very good at it.

One lunchtime, when Mum was just heading out for work, Milly slipped round her legs, aiming for the open door. But Mum swooped down and caught her just before she could escape.

"No, sweetie. I know you don't like staying inside, but it's to keep you safe." Mum sighed. "Hopefully the police will catch those awful cat thieves soon. It's been weeks. You stay there, and I'll be back later with Tia and Christy."

Crossly, Milly prowled back into the living room and jumped up on to the windowsill, watching Mum hurry away down the street. She hated it when they all went out. There was nothing to do. The cat on the other side of the road wasn't even sitting in his window for her to look at.

And she was hungry. She uncurled herself, jumped down and wandered out into the kitchen to see if there was some food left in her bowl. There wasn't.

Milly stalked over to the cat flap and glared at it. She didn't understand why it didn't work any more. It would let her back in from the garden, but now it would never let her out. She pawed at it, just in case, but it still didn't work. It rattled though, which was a good noise, so Milly pawed it again. This time, the catflap shook, and Milly got a delicious whiff of fresh garden air as the flap opened inwards a little way. Then it clicked shut again.

Milly stared at it. It had definitely been a bit open. She banged at it harder this time, and it flew open a little more.

Enough for her to stick her paw in and stop it clicking closed.

Purring with excitement, the kitten wriggled her other paw into the gap and then poked her nose in too, flipping the cat flap all the way up, so she could jump out. She stared back at it triumphantly as she stood on the doorstep, and then she pranced out into the garden.

It was sunny and warm, and everything smelled good. Milly padded across the patio, sniffing here and there, and glancing up at the birds that circled and twittered overhead.

193

It was the smell of the wheelie bins that made her go down the side path. She was hungry, and although the smell wasn't quite right, there was definitely food in there somewhere. She pattered curiously down the path and sniffed around the bottom of the bins. She was just considering trying to scramble up on to the top of one when next-door's dog, Max, came galloping down the garden on his side of the fence, barking his head off.

Milly shot down the path like a rocket, her tail fluffing up. She remembered Max, all big teeth and flying ears. She wasn't sure if he could get through the fence, but she wasn't going to wait around to find out. She bounded into the front garden and jumped up on to the wall. She then licked her paws furiously, swiping them over her ears. She felt hot and bothered and cross, and washing helped – a little.

The sun was warm, and slowly her tail smoothed down again. Milly's eyes half-closed as she watched the cars going past.

One of the cars stopped, a blue van that she was sure she had seen before. A young man with blond hair got out. Milly pricked up her ears. She had seen him before. He always stopped to admire her in the window. She pretended not to notice the man as he walked up the street, and she gave him a haughty look as he made friendly kissy noises at her.

But she couldn't hold out for long.

She padded gracefully down the wall

to let the man stroke her ears and tickle her under the chin.

Milly didn't even mind when he picked her up – she liked to be cuddled.

But then he locked his hand tightly around the scruff of her neck and hurried down the road with her. He opened the back of his blue van and stuffed her into a cat carrier.

And then he drove away while Milly howled and scrabbled and fought to get out.

Chapter Five

"Oh! Milly isn't in the window," Tia said, sounding surprised.

"Maybe she heard Christy singing and went to the door already," Mum suggested. "I bet the whole street heard her."

But there was no kitten rubbing lovingly around their ankles when Mum opened the front door.

Tia hurried into the kitchen to see if Milly was waiting by her food bowl. There was no sign of her at all. "Where is she?" she asked anxiously. "Did you shut her in upstairs, Mum?"

"No... She was definitely getting under my feet when I left," Mum said. "Unless she managed to shut herself in somewhere. Go and check, you two."

Tia and Christy raced upstairs, opening every door and calling frantically. Tia even looked in their wardrobe.

"Milly won't be in there!" Christy told her, but Tia shook her head.

"You never know. Remember when she got shut in the kitchen cupboard?"

"She only went in there because that's where the bag of cat food is,"

Christy pointed out.

But all the cupboards were empty, and they hurried back downstairs.

Mum was starting to get worried. "I've looked everywhere down here," she murmured. "You didn't unlock the cat flap, did you?"

Tia shook her head, glancing at the cat flap. Then she frowned. "Hey, it's not closed properly." She crouched down next to it. It was definitely open, just a little – the flap balanced against the frame. Tia gulped. "She's gone out."

"But it was locked," Mum protested. "How can she have gone out?"

"Look." Tia pointed. "It's still locked, but the lock's only a bit of plastic, Mum. It stops the door opening out, but Milly's so clever, she didn't open it outwards – she pulled it *in*. And then she squeezed under the flap."

Tia unlocked the back door and ran out into the garden. "Milly! Milly!" she called, hoping to see a toffee-gold kitten come darting through the grass. But all she heard was Max, whining next door.

"She's gone..." Tia whispered, her heart thumping so hard it almost hurt. "Someone's taken her." She knew that it was silly – Milly could be in Mr Jackson's garden again, chasing the fish. Or messing about in that garden with all the brambles a few doors down. There was nothing to say that she'd been catnapped. But somehow Tia knew. She just knew.

Milly peered out of the wire cage. The man had tipped her out of the carrier, and she had felt so dazed and dizzy after the car journey that she had simply curled up in the corner with her eyes shut. But now that she was feeling a little better she was trying to understand where she was and what was happening.

Her cage was small – not all that much bigger than the carrier had been – and there was a tatty blanket in it, a litter tray and a water bowl. There was a food bowl, too, but it was empty. The cage was stacked on top of another one and there were several more all round the shed. The whole place was grubby and cold, and it smelled as though the litter trays weren't emptied often enough. It was dark, too – the only window was dirty and hardly let in any light.

But the strangest thing was that there were three other cats. Milly hadn't seen that many since she'd come to live with Tia and Christy. Occasionally she would see one of the neighbourhood cats prowling through her garden, which she hated. But there wasn't a lot she could do about it, except scrabble her paws on the window.

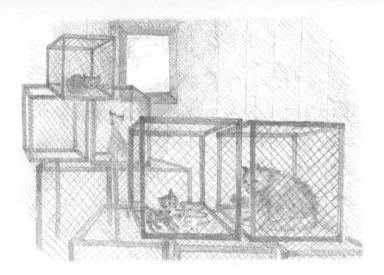

There was a cat in the cage right next to her, just on the other side of the wire. He was bigger than her, and he had a fat, squashed face and a lot of long fur in a strange blue-grey colour. He hissed angrily at Milly, and she took a step back and nearly fell over.

The big blue Persian hissed again and shot out a fat paw, scraping it down the side of the wire with a screechy clatter.

Milly's tail fluffed up to twice its usual size, and she hissed and spat back. She might be small, but she was angry.

She had been stolen and stuffed in a box, and now she was shut up here.

The Persian was still hissing, but crawling backwards now, his golden-orange eyes fixed on hers. They glared at each other, both of them refusing to back down.

As Milly watched him edge up against the side of his cage she decided that there wasn't much point in making a fuss. He was there and she was here, neither of them could get out – that was what they should be worrying about.

She let out a last little growl and curled herself up on the blanket, wondering how she was going to get home to Tia.

"Anything?" Mum asked, as Tia came in from the garden. She had been out to call for Milly again while Mum and Christy went to ask Mr Jackson if he'd seen the kitten, and Max's owners too. No one had seen her, though.

Tia rubbed her eyes, trying not to cry. She didn't want to scare Christy. "Do you think someone took her?" she whispered to Mum.

Mum hugged her. "No, Tia, I'm sure she's just gone exploring. Don't worry."

But Tia *was* worried. Milly never went far. Whenever Tia called her, there'd always be a scrabbling on the other side of the fence and a little whiskery golden face would appear over the top. "Can we go and look up and down the road?" she begged.

They searched their street and the next couple of streets, calling for Milly and asking people if they'd spotted her. And they kept going until it got too dark to see.

Mum said Milly would probably come back when she got hungry, but the kitten still hadn't returned by bedtime. Christy climbed the ladder to Tia's top bunk, and the sisters curled up together.

"She'll come back tomorrow, won't she?" Christy asked.

Tia tried to sound confident. "Oh yes." *Please let it be true*, she thought. "We'll probably find her in her basket when we come down in the morning."

"She could be there now!" Christy clutched at Tia's pyjamas. "We should go downstairs and see!"

"No… Not yet," Tia murmured. She wasn't sure she could manage not to cry if they didn't find their lovely kitten.

"I really miss her…" Christy said sleepily.

"Me too," Tia sniffed. "But she'll be back tomorrow," she said, trying to convince herself.

Chapter Six

But the next morning there was no Milly yowling for her breakfast. It seemed so unfair to have to go to school – all Tia wanted to do was search for Milly. It was Friday. Nothing important happened at school on Fridays.

As she trailed into the playground, her friend Lucy came running over.

"Hi, Tia! Hey, what's the matter?"

"Milly," Tia gulped, swallowing back tears. "She's disappeared. And I can't help thinking someone's kidnapped her. Remember I told you about those cat thieves?"

Lucy's eyes widened. "Oh no! How long's she been gone for?"

"She wasn't there when we got home yesterday. She managed to get out of her cat flap even though it was locked."

Lucy frowned. "I don't think Mittens would ever do anything like that. What makes you think she's been stolen?"

Tia sighed. "It's just a feeling I've got... I know that sounds stupid."

"No..." Lucy said thoughtfully. "I know what you mean. When Mittens was lost, I was sure she'd come back. She was gone for more than a week, and

Mum told me maybe I should give up, but I didn't."

"I forgot about that! It was in the summer holidays, wasn't it? How did you find her?" Tia asked eagerly.

"We made loads of posters and stuck them on lamp posts, and I put leaflets through the door of every house in our road, asking them to check their sheds. And that's where somebody found her! It was just lucky that it was a leaky shed and there was a puddle of water, otherwise Mittens would have died," Lucy added, her voice shaking a little.

"Posters…" Tia said thoughtfully. "And leaflets. Right. We'll make some tonight."

"What about this one?" Tia said to Dad, pointing to one of the photos of Milly on the screen.

"Mmmm." Dad nodded. "But she's more recognizable from the side, don't you think? Because of her lovely spots."

"Look!" Christy said. "That's the one Mum took when Milly climbed into the cupboard!"

Tia enlarged the photo and smiled. Milly was peering out, looking worried. They'd actually moved the cat food to the top cupboard after her first cat-food raid. And Mum had even started keeping the food in a tin instead of a bag. But Milly was just too clever. She'd even managed to hook the lid open with her claws.

"She's so naughty…" Mum sighed.

"Mum!" Tia looked up at her. "Aren't you sad she's missing?"

"Of course I am, Tia! But she *is* naughty!"

"I suppose you wish we had a better-behaved cat instead!" Tia said, her voice choked with tears.

"I didn't mean that at all," Mum tried to say, but Tia was too upset to listen.

"You're glad she's gone!" she sobbed.

"Tia!" Mum snapped, her voice sharp

enough to jolt Tia out of her fit of crying. "Sweetheart, that's just silly. Yes, I get cross with Milly when she's naughty, but she's a kitten! Kittens do silly things, it's what we signed up for! Especially when we agreed to have a Bengal." She put her arm round Tia's shoulder. "Do you think you're the only one who read that book on Bengal cats?"

Tia gaped at her. She hadn't realized Mum had read the book too.

"When I'm at home with her in the mornings, she follows me around, you know." Mum sniffed. "And I'm always having to rescue her from the washing machine. It's a wonder I've never actually put it on with her in it! I love her too, Tia, and we will do our absolute best to find her."

"Sorry," Tia murmured. Somehow knowing that Mum was really missing Milly helped.

Dad smiled. "She's a little terror, isn't she? But nobody wants a better-behaved cat, Tia. We want *our* cat. Now I think this photo of her in the garden is the best. What shall we say on the poster?"

Milly stared at the door, wondering when the man would come to bring their food. He'd fed them that morning, but the food hadn't been the same kind she had at home. She'd left it for a while, but then finally eaten it – she'd been too hungry not to.

214

She had tried to dart out of the cage when the man put her food bowl in, but he'd batted her away. She felt hopeless – she couldn't see how she was ever going to get out of here. And she was hungry again.

Tia always fed her at about this time of day. Where *was* Tia? Milly had been hoping that Tia would come and take her away from this horrible place.

She began to wail, over and over again. The Persian cat didn't join in, he just stayed in the corner of his cage, sulking. But the other two cats started to howl too.

The door banged open, and the man stamped in, scowling. "Shut up!" he yelled, hitting the front of the cage.

Milly let out a frightened little whimper. No one had ever shouted at her like that before. People had been cross or snapped, "Milly, no!" But this was different. She cowered at the back of the cage as he shoved in a fresh bowl of food. She didn't even think about trying to escape this time. She didn't want to go any closer to the man than she had to.

"I'm glad it's Saturday and we can be out looking for Milly," Tia said to Lucy. Her mum had texted Lucy's the night before to ask if Lucy could come and help.

"That's a brilliant photo," Lucy said, as she gave Tia some sellotape to stick the poster to a lamp post. "Anyone who sees Milly will definitely recognize her."

Tia sighed. "I don't think anyone will see her, though. I still reckon it was those catnappers Laura told me about. Mum did ring the police, and they said they'd make a note of it, but there wasn't a lot to go on. Actually, do you mind if we run back and ask Mum if we can go and tell Laura what's happened? I want to warn her to keep Charlie safe."

"Good idea," Lucy agreed. "If the catnappers did take Milly, I bet they saw Charlie too. They might come back, mightn't they?"

"Exactly." Tia shuddered.

They hurried back down the road to meet Tia's mum and Christy, who were doing the lamp posts at that end. Mum had told the girls they could go further up the road as long as they stayed where she could see them. Dad had gone to the street that ran behind theirs, in case Milly had jumped over the back fence.

"Mum! Can we go and tell Laura what happened? I want to warn her to keep Charlie in."

"Oh, Tia… I'm sure it's nothing to do with catnappers," Mum said, patting her shoulder. "Milly's just wandered off. Cats do!"

"Please?"

"Well, OK. But don't bother Laura for long."

Tia and Lucy crossed over the road, and rang Laura's bell.

"Hello! I've just seen you from upstairs, putting up posters." Laura frowned. "Milly's not lost, is she?"

"Yes." Tia gulped. "Actually, I'm sure

she's been stolen. There was a man asking me about her, just a couple of days ago…"

Laura gasped. "Youngish? Short blond hair? With a blue van?"

"I don't know about the van…" Tia started to say. "Hang on, yes, there was a van…" She scowled to herself, wishing she could remember. It just hadn't seemed important at the time. "I think it was blue. You saw him too, then?"

"Yes! He was asking me about Charlie. He was nice, he said my cat looked very special, and I was all set to say Charlie was a Bengal. Then I remembered that newspaper article, and I just smiled at him and went inside. I felt a bit guilty afterwards. I was rude…"

"He was nice to me too," Tia whispered sadly. "If he was asking about Charlie, that's not just chance, is it? He's a cat thief, and Milly really has been stolen." Tia's eyes filled with tears. "He'll sell her to someone else, and we'll never get her back!"

Chapter Seven

Milly flattened her ears. She could hear the man coming. She gave a small, nervous mew. He frightened her.

He had a pile of food bowls in one hand, but in the other he was holding a cat carrier. What was happening? Then she suddenly realized – perhaps he was going to take her home! She purred, hoping she was the one he had brought the carrier for.

She stood nicely as he opened the cage door, and let him pick her up and put her in, though usually she would scrabble and fight.

"Who's being a good girl," he murmured in the sort of voice that Tia would use. Milly still didn't like him, but at least he was carrying her carefully. She had expected him to put her back in the van. But instead he put the carrier down indoors somewhere and left her.

What was happening? Why had he put her in the carrier if he wasn't going to take her home? Milly mewed worriedly, but she didn't howl like she had before. If she was noisy, she was sure the man would shout at her again.

At last, she heard him coming back.

He was talking to someone else, a woman, and his voice was soft.

"Yes, she's lovely. Unfortunately her owner couldn't keep her. The old lady had to go into hospital, you see, so she asked me to find her a new home. She's very reasonably priced for a Bengal."

Milly tensed as he undid the clips on the front door of the carrier, and then he reached in and scooped her out. She did her best not to hiss, but she wanted to, and the fur rose up all along her back.

"Oh dear, she doesn't look very happy." The woman frowned. "She's so pretty, though. Do you have her pedigree?"

"I don't have the pedigree at the moment – with being in hospital, her owner was a bit frantic. But it's very good."

"Can I hold her?" the woman asked, and she took Milly, stroking her softly. The woman seemed nice – or at any rate, a lot nicer than the man. Milly relaxed a little. She didn't know who this person was, but perhaps she was going to take her back to Tia.

"Oh…" The lady ran her hand down Milly's tail. "There's something wrong with her tail."

"What?" The man's voice was cross

225

again, and Milly flinched and pressed herself against the woman's coat.

"Look – it's bent over."

"Well, that doesn't matter, does it? Seeing how reasonable the price is."

"I don't know. If there's something wrong with her..." The woman held Milly out to the man. "I hope I haven't wasted your time."

Milly looked up at her, realizing that she wasn't going to take her away from here, and let out a despairing yowl. The man snatched her and stuffed her into the carrier, slamming the wire door angrily. He looked furious – and the woman appeared very glad to be leaving.

Milly was worried that he might come back and shout at her again. But there was a loud bang, like a door shutting, and heavy footsteps went thudding away upstairs.

After a few minutes she felt brave enough to come closer to the wire door and look out. The room was a kitchen, a bit like Tia's, and the carrier seemed to be on a table. Milly pressed her nose up against the wire and then jumped back as it moved.

He hadn't shut the door! He had only slammed it – he hadn't twisted the catches to hold it in place! Milly nudged the door with her nose, harder and harder, and it swung open. She jumped out on to the table. She had to get away from here, as quickly as she could. She looked over at the back door, but there was no cat flap.

There was a window, though. Above the sink, like at home. And it was open, just a little.

Milly stood at the edge of the table, her back legs tensed, ready to spring. There were glasses and plates stacked by the sink, and if she banged into them, he might come. She had to be quiet as well as quick. She leaped right into the sink, and some knives and forks jingled under her paws. But there was no thunder of footsteps on the stairs. Hurriedly, she climbed up to the windowsill. She was free!

"What did the police say?" Tia asked. She'd been hovering by her mum the whole while she'd been on the phone.

"Well, this time they did seem to take it a bit more seriously. They said they'd pass on all the information."

"They think Milly *was* stolen, then?" Tia said, her voice eager. "They'll find her?"

Mum sighed. "Look, Tia, the police will do the best they can. But there isn't a lot to go on, is there?"

"I suppose not," Tia sat down at the table, her legs feeling wobbly. Then she frowned. "If they haven't got much to go on, we have to find them some more evidence, Mum! Lucy said we should put posters up in the shops near her. There's a newsagent's with a board – she says loads of people go and read the ads on it. Please!"

"All right. It's quite a walk, though. Dad's taken the car to drive round and look for Milly."

"I don't mind!" Tia assured her.

Mum sighed. "Have you printed out some more posters?"

Tia picked up a pile from the end of the table and waved them at her.

"Now, you two go into the newsagent's, and I'll go and ask if I can put a poster up in the library," Mum said. She was sounding a bit weary. Christy had whinged most of the way, saying she was sick of walking. Tia had tried to explain that it was all because they were trying to find Milly, but when Christy was tired she wasn't easy to persuade.

Tia walked up to the counter and the young woman smiled at her. "Are you after some sweets?" she asked.

Tia shook her head. "We came to ask if we could put this up on your board." She held out a poster. "It's our kitten, you see. She's missing."

"Oh no! Look at her, isn't she lovely!"

Tia swallowed back tears. "We think she might have been stolen. There was an article about it in the local paper."

"I remember. Is your cat one of those Bengals, then?"

"Yes. A man was hanging around asking about her, and one day we got back home from school and she was gone."

The woman nodded. "The board's over there. You can move a couple of the leaflets around if you need space."

"Thank you very much!" Tia went over to the board while Christy eyed the sweets hungrily. It was covered in leaflets, some of them curling at the edges as though they'd been there forever. Tia started to unpin a few of them so she could make room for her poster. Most of them were adverts for things people wanted to sell – lawnmowers and pushchairs. Then Tia stopped, staring at the card she'd just taken down.

Pedigree cats for sale. All breeds. Reasonably priced.

And there was a phone number.

How could someone be selling all breeds of cat? Breeders like Helen only bred one sort. No one could have all the different breeds.

Unless they were stealing them.

"What's the matter?" the woman called to Tia. "You look like you've seen a ghost."

Tia walked back over to the counter. "You don't remember who put this up, do you?" she asked, not very hopefully.

The woman looked down at the card. "Oh, I see. You're thinking—"

"It could be them, couldn't it?" Tia gasped. She was desperate for a clue. Anything that might help them track Milly down.

The woman sniffed. "As it happens, I do know who put that up, and I wouldn't be surprised if he *was* a cat thief. He's rude. I wish he didn't come in here, but he picks up his motorcycle magazine every week. Some special order."

Tia stared at her. "So – have you got his address then?" she whispered.

The woman looked uncomfortable. "Well, yes… I mean, I shouldn't give it out. Just don't say I gave it to you, will you?" She pulled out a big folder and flicked through. "Here, look. That's him. But hang on, you can't go over there on your own! Where's your mum and dad?"

"It's all right," Tia said. "My mum's just at the library – I'll get her. Seventeen Emwell Road. Thanks!"

She grabbed Christy's hand, and hauled her out of the shop. "I think we're about to get Milly back! We have to find Mum… Come on."

They raced up the steps to the library and shoved open the door. Mum was in the queue, and there were loads of people in front of her.

"I won't be too long, Tia," Mum said, as Tia came up to her.

"But I've found them!" Tia cried. "The catnappers!"

"What?" Mum stared at her, and some of the people in the line looked round curiously.

"There was an ad for pedigree cats for sale in the newsagent's. It has to be them! And I've got the address."

"Oh, Tia, I know you're desperate to find Milly, but you're jumping to conclusions." Mum shook her head.

"Why won't you ever believe me?" Tia said furiously. "I'm going there now!" She turned and marched out, Christy scampering after her. She didn't even look back to see if Mum was following. She just had to find Milly.

Chapter Eight

Milly threaded her way through the overgrown front garden and squeezed under the rickety wooden gate. She darted a glance back to the house, but the man wasn't chasing her. Still, she wanted to get further away. Then she would find Tia. She set off down the pavement, sniffing at the dandelions and the parked cars. It was when she reached the end of the street, where it met another, larger road, that she realized finding her home was going to be harder than she'd thought. She had expected to somehow know which way to go. But coming here in a van, she had lost her sense of direction.

She set off along one road, but it didn't feel good. Milly turned uncertainly and hurried back. The other way felt as though it led home.

Milly plodded on, trying to sense the right direction. She wasn't used to walking so far and the pavements were hard. Her paws hurt. Worst of all, she wasn't really sure she was getting any closer to Tia.

Wearily, she jumped up on to a low wall for a rest. Another cat had scent-marked the garden beyond the wall, and Milly peered down nervously. The cat didn't seem to be around. She curled herself into a tense little ball and let her eyes close. She was so tired.

Suddenly, Milly's eyes shot open, and she nearly fell off the wall. A ginger cat was in the garden below her, hissing furiously. His fur fluffed up so much that he looked four times as big as her.

Milly scrambled backwards, her tail straight up, all the fur sticking out like a brush. She hissed at the ginger cat, but he was much bigger than she was. Milly backed herself up to the end of the wall and then sprang down on to the pavement, racing away as fast as she could.

"It's this way," Tia panted, hauling Christy along behind her.

"We should wait for Mum!" Christy wailed. "I can't see her, Tia! We aren't supposed to go where we can't see Mum! We'll get in trouble!"

"I don't care! I'm going to find Milly. Look, this is Emwell Road!"

Tia stopped, gasping for breath. What if the man who took Milly saw her and Christy? He'd probably recognize them. "Be like spies, all right? We don't want the catnappers to catch us."

Tia pulled Christy in close to the wall and they began to creep along, looking for number seventeen.

"This is it," Tia murmured, a little way up the road. "Oh! The van!" She squeezed Christy's hand and pointed. "Laura saw a blue van when the man was asking about Charlie."

"Tia!" Mum was running up the road after them, looking furious. "How could you run off like that? You crossed roads! You know you're not allowed!"

"Mum, look!" Tia grabbed her arm, towing her towards the van. "Look! It's the catnappers!"

Mum frowned. "Oh… Is that the van Laura talked about?"

"Yes! And this is the road where the man who put up that advert lives. It's got to be him, hasn't it?"

Mum nodded slowly. "All right. Don't you dare go in there, Tia! I'm going to call that number the police gave me. It's starting to look as though you're right."

"Have a look at these." The policewoman held out her mobile phone, and Tia stared at it eagerly. It had been so hard to wait for news. Tia had wanted to stay outside the house in Emwell Road, but Mum had said they'd better go home. They didn't want to get in the way when the police came.

"We might make that man suspicious if we're hanging around," she had pointed out to Tia. "We don't want him moving the cats."

Tia knew she was right, but she hated to walk away when she was so sure that Milly was somewhere in that house.

It had only been a few hours until a police car drew up outside their house that evening, but it felt like Tia had been waiting for days.

"Is Milly one of these?" PC Ryan flicked through the photos – a Persian, and what looked like another Bengal, but with a marbled, stripey coat, and another cat Tia didn't recognize.

"No..." Tia's voice shook. "Look, there's an empty cage next to this one. He's already sold her!"

PC Ryan frowned. "Maybe. But he was definitely showing a spotted Bengal kitten to someone this morning. Another lady phoned us, saying that she'd been to see a kitten, and she suspected she might have been stolen. Perhaps your Milly got out."

"Milly is very good at getting in and out of places," Mum agreed hopefully. "If any cat could, it would be her, wouldn't it, Tia..."

But Tia wasn't listening. She dashed away upstairs to her room and scrambled up her ladder to hide in her bed. She couldn't bear it. They were too late, and Milly was gone.

Milly kept walking all afternoon even though she was so tired she stumbled. The light was starting to fade now, and it was getting colder. Someone was walking along the road towards her with a dog, and Milly darted under a parked car to hide.

Even when the dog had gone by, she didn't want to move. At least under the car she was out of the wind, and she couldn't smell any other cats. She would just stay here for a little while, until she felt better. Milly dozed, her eyelids flickering and her paws twitching as the ginger cat chased after her. It was chasing her further and further away from Tia...

She hissed and startled awake, not sure where she was. It was now bright daylight, she realized as she peered out from under the parked car. She must have slept there all night, worn out from her long walk.

She stepped cautiously out on to the pavement and stretched herself. Then she heard voices. Children's voices. Not Tia and Christy, she was pretty sure, but still … she would just go and see. Somehow she felt much more hopeful today, with the bright sunshine warming her fur.

It was a playground, and two little boys were chasing each other round and round. Milly paused at the gate, ready to run.

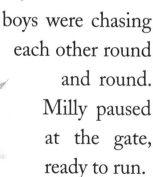

"Ooooh, look! Mum, look! A kitten!" The older boy dashed over.

Milly squeaked – she was nervous after the way that nice man had turned out not to be nice after all. She shot underneath the slide and hid there, shivering.

"Oh, Alfie, you frightened her. She doesn't know you like Whiskers does. No, don't try and pull her out, Billy. She'll come out if she wants to."

The woman's voice was gentle, and the fur began to lay down flat on Milly's back again. "She is pretty… Oh!"

"What, Mum?"

"I think she's the kitten on those posters! You know, we said it was sad that she was lost. She's called Milly, if she is that missing kitten."

249

"And we found her!"

"No, I found her! I saw her first!"

"Shhh! You'll scare her away. We need to ring the number and say she's found. You two watch her, and I'll run and see if I can find a poster. I think I saw one on that lamp post by the gate."

Milly huddled under the slide with two curious little faces staring in. She was feeling a bit better now – the bigger boy had surprised her, that was all. She sniffed at his fingers as he held them out hopefully, and he beamed and patted her head.

"Hello, Milly..."

Milly came out from under the slide a little more. The boy knew her name! She nuzzled his fingers, and he giggled.

"Me too! Me too!" the littler one

squeaked, so she rubbed her head against his jeans.

The boys' mother hurried back over. "Good boys... I'm just ringing her owners now..." she said, crouching down beside them. She smiled at Milly as she keyed in the number. "I bet you want to go home, don't you?"

"Tia, love, wake up."

Tia blinked and rubbed at her sticky eyes. They were sore, and she couldn't remember why. And then all at once she did remember and she gave a horrified little gasp.

Mum was standing at the bottom of the bunkbed ladder with Christy next to her. "Tia, why don't you get up and have a shower and get changed? You fell asleep in your clothes last night!"

Tia peered over the edge of her bed. "Milly could be anywhere, Mum. That man isn't telling the police anything, PC Ryan said so. He just says he's looking after the cats for a friend. He must have sold her. We're never going

252

to get Milly back."

"Listen, Dad and I think PC Ryan's right. The man was showing someone a kitten just like Milly yesterday morning. You *know* how sneaky Milly can be! She ran away from him, I'm sure she did. The police have arrested the man, so they'll be able to ask him more questions. Dad's gone to put more posters up around Emwell Road. Do you want to go out looking again after breakfast? Shall we see if Lucy wants to come and help too?"

Tia sniffed and nodded, and Mum reached up awkwardly to hug her round the ladder. "Oh, that's my phone. Maybe it's Dad." She dug it out of her pocket. "Hello?" She listened for a moment and then she gasped, shaking

Tia's shoulder. "Someone's found her! She *must* have escaped! She's not even that far away." Mum held the phone back to her ear. "In the park between here and school. Oh, thank you so much, we'll be there in a few minutes. Tia, come back!"

But Tia had already jumped down the ladder, and Christy was racing after her.

Milly had stopped listening to the little boys as they told her how nice she was and what soft fur she had. She could hear something. A voice…

It was Christy! "Tia, wait for me!"

"Come on, Christy! This is where Milly is, they said on the phone."

Milly jumped right over the little boy's knees and raced for the park gate.

"She's there! Look!" Christy squealed.

"Milly!" Tia crouched down and the kitten bounded up to her, purring delightedly. "Oh, we were so worried!" She stood up, cradling Milly in her arms like a baby.

"Thank you for phoning us!" Tia said shyly to the woman with the two little boys.

The woman smiled. "I'm just glad we saw her. She's beautiful, isn't she?"

Tia smiled back. "She's the most beautiful kitten ever."

Christy danced round her sister. "We found you! Mum, look, here's Milly!"

"She's fine!" Tia called, as she turned to see Mum hurrying towards them.

"Better than fine," her mum said, gently tickling Milly under the chin. "You little darling, did you run away from that man, hmmm?"

"The most beautiful kitten ever *and* the cleverest!" Tia sighed happily. It felt like she could breathe properly for the first time since Milly had disappeared. There had been a horrible lump of fear stuck in her throat all that time. "We got you back," she whispered, rubbing her cheek over the top of the kitten's head, and Milly purred so hard she shook all over.

Lucky Escape for Kidnapped Kitten!

Reunited: Tia and Christy are delighted to have their kitten back!

A Bengal kitten was returned to her owners after escaping from the clutches of a local cat thief. The cat, named Milly, was stolen last week. The thief intended to sell her to unsuspecting customers.

Fortunately, her dedicated owner, Tia, put up posters and undertook detective work following our recent article about catnapping. Milly was found at a local playground, having somehow escaped from the thief. And, thanks to the posters, the lady who found her knew who to call!

Tia and her younger sister, Christy, were thrilled to have Milly returned safely. As Tia told *The Purberry Post*: "I was so frightened when she went missing, but I suppose I should have known she'd escape the catnapper – she's so clever!"

The thief has been caught and is under questioning by the police. Three other pedigree cats found at his home have been returned to their rightful owners.

The
Frightened
Kitten

For Lara

Chapter One

"Make sure you wrap it up carefully," Kate told Maddy, stuffing an armful of bubble wrap into her best friend's lap.

Maddy nodded, smoothing it out and starting to wind it round the photo frame. "Ben looks gorgeous in this picture," she said, her voice a bit wobbly.

Kate nodded. "He always does. But that's my favourite photo of him."

Maddy stared down at the photo – she was in it too. It had been taken last summer, and showed her and Kate, with Kate's huge black cat Ben sitting on the picnic rug between them. He was almost as tall as they were, when the girls were sitting down.

She laughed with surprise as a hard head butted her arm, and Ben stomped his way on to her lap to see exactly what she was doing. He'd been asleep at the end of Kate's bed, but he'd obviously decided something interesting was happening. He was the world's nosiest cat.

"Do you think he'll mind moving?" Maddy asked, watching Kate fill a big cardboard box with books and her ornaments, all carefully wrapped up.

"I don't know." Kate shrugged. "The new house has got a big garden, but he likes it here. Like me." She sighed miserably. "I keep hoping Dad's going to come home and say it was all a mistake, and he doesn't have to go and work in Yorkshire after all. But we're leaving tomorrow. It's getting a bit late for that." She sniffed, and sat down next to Maddy and Ben on the bed.

Maddy put an arm round her, and Ben bounced on to Kate's lap, standing up on his hind legs to wrap his front paws around her neck. It was his party trick. Kate always told people she had a cat who hugged, although he didn't do it to very many people. Mostly Kate, but he would do it to Maddy sometimes, especially if she'd given him a cat treat. He'd even done it to Maddy's dad once, when he came to pick Maddy up and stopped for a cup of tea. Her dad had been taken by surprise, but Maddy had noticed that he always looked for Ben whenever he came to Kate's now. As though he was hoping that Ben might do it again.

Maddy had been working on her mum and dad to let her get a cat of her own for ages. She was pretty sure that Ben had won her dad over that day. Now she just had to persuade her mum…

Kate sniffed again. "What if he doesn't like the new house, Maddy? He might even try and find his way back here. You read in the papers about cats who do that."

"Yorkshire's probably too far for him to try it," Maddy said. It was meant to be comforting, but it didn't work. She didn't want to think about how far away her friend was going to be. And she was going to have to start a new school, of course. Maddy couldn't imagine having to do that.

Kate frowned. "I hope there aren't too many other cats near the new house.

Ben's the top cat round here, none of the other cats would put a paw in our garden. But the new garden might be another cat's territory already."

Maddy looked down at Ben, now sitting comfortably on Kate's lap. He yawned and stretched, and then stared up at her with huge green eyes. *He* didn't look like he was worried.

"Even if the garden is another cat's territory, I don't think it will be for long," Maddy said, stroking him.

Kate nodded, laughing. "Maybe. He doesn't fight very often, but when he does, I think he just sits on the other cats and squashes them." She sighed. "I suppose I'd better get on with packing. Mum says I should have had it finished yesterday." She pushed Ben gently off her knee, and he slunk away to hide among the boxes.

Maddy went back to wrapping up the photo. She was going to miss Kate so much. She knew Kate would miss her too, but her friend was a bit like Ben, Maddy thought. She was so strong and bouncy and confident. She'd have a new gang of friends in no time – and she'd be showing off her famous hugging cat to them instead.

"Pass me that tape, Maddy, so I can seal this box up."

Maddy handed her the parcel tape, and wrapped another photo frame. "Where did Ben go?" she asked, a few minutes later.

"He's under the bed, isn't he?" Kate said, peering down.

But he wasn't. There was a sudden thumping and then a muffled yowl. "He's in the box!" Maddy giggled.

Kate stared at the big cardboard box she'd just taped up. "He can't be…" she murmured, but she didn't sound very sure. She ripped off the tape, and the flaps came up, followed by a large black head, with cross, glowing green eyes. Ben scrambled out, hissing grumpily.

"Well, you shouldn't have been in there!" Kate laughed. "Nosy boy!"

Maddy was laughing too. But even as she laughed, she was thinking, *I'm going to miss them so much…*

Kate and her mum walked Maddy home – it was only five minutes away, and it was warm and sunny. Perfect Easter holiday weather. If Kate hadn't been leaving tomorrow, they'd have spent loads of time in the park, or maybe gone out somewhere for the day.

"Those cats that live next door to you are nearly as big as Ben," Kate's mum commented, as they came up to Maddy's garden.

"They're sitting on Mum's daffodils again," Maddy sighed, as she hurried into the front garden and tried to shoo the two big ginger cats off the stone pot that her mum had planted full of bulbs. For some reason Tiger and Tom had decided it was a really good place to sit, and the daffodils were looking a bit squashed now.

Maddy's mum opened the front door. "I heard you coming, girls. Oh, no, not those horrible cats again!"

Tiger spat crossly at Maddy as she tried to get him off the daffodils, and yowled. He was so different to lovely, sweet-natured Ben. At last, he jumped down, and the pair of them stalked away, glaring back at Maddy.

As the mums chatted, Kate flung her arms round Maddy. "Promise you'll call me every day! Tell me everything that's happening at school, OK?"

Maddy nodded. "And anyway, you're coming back to visit at half-term."

"We'd better go," Kate's mum said. "It'll be a long day tomorrow, and there's still some packing to do."

And that was it. Kate and her mum went back down the path, waving, and Maddy was left on her own.

"I've finished," said Maddy, pushing away her half-eaten dinner. Mum had made her favourite pasta, but she just wasn't hungry.

Her dad leaned over and put an arm round her shoulders. "Do you think we could tell her the news? To cheer her up?" he suggested to Maddy's mum, and she nodded.

"What news?" Maddy sniffed sadly.

"Do you remember me telling you that my friend Donna's cat had kittens a couple of months ago?" Mum asked.

"Oh, yes. You showed me a photo on your phone. They're gorgeous. There were some tortoiseshell ones – my favourite kind!"

"Good. Because one of them is going to be yours!"

Maddy blinked. "I'm getting a kitten?"

"You can choose which of the litter you'd like. Donna needs to find homes for them all, and we thought it would be nice for you to have a cat, as you've wanted one for so long. Especially as you're bound to miss Kate – getting to know a kitten might make the Easter holidays a bit less sad." Her mum looked at her anxiously. "We're not trying to take your mind off missing her, Maddy. It's a really sad thing for a friend to move away."

"It just seemed like a good time," her dad added.

Maddy nodded. "It is a good time," she whispered. She couldn't help still feeling sad about Kate, of course, but at the same time, inside she was jumping about and squeaking. *A kitten! A kitten! I'm getting a kitten!*

Chapter Two

Maddy's mum showed her some more photos of the kittens, but it was hard to see them in the pictures on her phone. Three of them were ginger and the other two were tortoiseshells, beautiful black, white and orange cats. They were all coiled and snuggled around each other and their mother, who was black like Ben. Maddy was pretty sure she would like a tortoiseshell kitten – Tiger and Tom had put her off ginger cats.

"When can I see them?" Maddy asked the next morning at breakfast.

Mum smiled. "I've arranged for us to visit them this afternoon. And if you're sure which kitten you'd like, you can even bring it home today! We can go to the pet shop on the way to Donna's house to get everything we'll need."

As it turned out, they needed an awful lot of things. A basket, Maddy had thought of that. And a food bowl. But she hadn't realized there was so much else. A collar. Grooming brush. Food. Special treats that were good for cleaning kitten teeth. Toys…

They were just about to go and pay for everything when Mum stopped.

"Oh, I'm so stupid! I forgot that Donna said to bring a cat carrier to take the kitten home in."

Maddy smiled. *Home!* She loved the idea of their house being a home for a kitten.

"If you get anything else, we won't have room for the kitten in the car," Dad muttered, but Maddy knew he was only joking.

"Can we go to Donna's now?" she said hopefully, as they stowed all the things in the boot a few minutes later.

Mum nodded, and hugged her. "I'm really excited."

Maddy threw her arms round her mum's neck. "I bet I'm more excited than you."

Dad got in the car and tooted the horn at them. "Come on. I'm so excited I actually want to go and see these kittens some time today!"

"Oh, look at them!" Maddy breathed, stopping in the kitchen doorway and staring. The kittens were all asleep in a large basket in the corner of the room. It was by the radiator, and the floor had been covered with newspaper.

"They're doing pretty well with their house-training; the newspaper's just in case they miss the litter tray," Donna explained. "We've been keeping them in the kitchen up till now, but this last week they keep on escaping!"

"How old are they?" Maddy asked. They looked so little. She couldn't believe they were ready to leave their mum.

"Ten weeks yesterday. I bought a book about raising kittens when we found out that Dilly was pregnant, and it recommended keeping them with their mum until then, so she can teach them what they need to know. Also, that way they get to spend more time with their brothers and sisters, and learn how to get on with each other."

"So did you mean for her to have kittens then?" Maddy's dad asked.

Donna sighed. "No, it was a total surprise. We were planning to have Dilly spayed, but we left it too late. As soon as she's recovered from having these, we'll take her to the vet. I love the kittens, but I don't want any more!"

"Are you going to keep any of them?" Maddy asked, as she knelt down by the basket. "I can't imagine how you're going to let them go, they're so gorgeous."

Donna nodded. "I know. I'd love to keep a couple, and it will be sad for Dilly to lose them all, but we only ever meant to have one cat! We'll have to see. Quite a few people seem interested in adopting one." She smiled at Maddy. "But you've got first choice. Your mum booked you a kitten weeks ago!"

Maddy looked up at her mum gratefully. "Thanks, Mum!"

"Well, it seemed like a perfect opportunity – you're old enough to help look after a pet now."

"I'll be really good, I promise," Maddy said. "I'll even clean out the litter tray." She wouldn't mind, she thought, peering into the basket. The kittens had heard their voices, and were starting to wake up. Dilly was watching Maddy carefully, obviously guarding her babies.

One of the ginger kittens popped its head up and stared curiously at Maddy. She laughed, and his eyes widened in surprise.

"Oh, sorry!" Maddy whispered. "I didn't mean to scare you."

All the kittens were awake now, gazing at her with big green eyes. Maddy sighed. "How am I ever going to choose one of you?" she murmured. She hadn't thought she'd like a ginger kitten, but they were cute too – their pink noses clashed with their orangey fur.

One of the tortoiseshell kittens put its paws up on the side of the basket, and nosed at Maddy's hand. Its nose felt chilly and tickly, and Maddy stifled a laugh. She didn't want to make the kitten jump.

"Is this a girl kitten?" she whispered to Donna. She'd guessed that the ginger kittens were boys and the tortoiseshells were girls, but she knew it wasn't always that way round.

"Yes, she's a sweetie. Very friendly, she loves to have her head rubbed."

The kitten looked at Maddy hopefully, and Maddy gently scratched  the top of her head. Ben had always liked that. The kitten purred, and turned her head sideways, nestling into Maddy's hand.

"She's lovely," Mum said quietly.

"Could we have her?" Maddy breathed. The kitten was still purring and cuddling up against her hand. She was so little and perfect. Maddy was desperate to pick her up, but she wasn't sure she should.

The kitten solved the problem by clambering over the side of the basket – it was a soft, squashy one, and the sides were so high that she looked like she was trying to climb over a bouncy castle. There was a lot of scrabbling, but eventually she landed on the kitchen floor, looking very proud of herself, and set to work mountaineering up on to Maddy's lap.

"Oooh, claws." Maddy giggled, and carefully scooped a hand under the kitten's bottom to give her a bit of a lift. The kitten finally reached her lap, looking quite worn out by the effort, but she purred delightedly when Maddy made a fuss of her.

"Well, it looks like she wants to be ours too," Dad said, reaching out a finger to scratch behind the kitten's ears. "What are we going to call her?"

Maddy looked down at the kitten, who was busily curling herself into a neat little ball. "See that orange patch on her back. It's completely round. Don't you think it looks just like a biscuit?"

"Biscuit?" Mum laughed. "That's a really cute name for a cat. It does look like a little ginger biscuit, against that white fur."

Maddy nodded. "It's the perfect name for her."

Maddy had the whole of the rest of the Easter holidays to get to know Biscuit, and play with her. Her mum and dad were right – having her kitten did mean she spent less time worrying about going back to school without Kate. She also did a lot of reading – they'd bought a book on cat care at the pet shop, and she got a couple more out of the library, too.

"Did Donna take the kittens to have their first vaccinations?" she asked Mum at breakfast, the day after they'd brought Biscuit home.

Biscuit was sitting on her lap, looking hopefully at Maddy's breakfast. The cereal looked quite like her cat biscuits, she thought, but it didn't smell the same. She reached up, stretching her neck, and sniffed harder. Definitely not cat biscuits, but a very good smell all the same. She put her front paws on the edge of the table, and darted her raspberry-pink tongue at a drop of milk that Maddy had spilled.

It was sweet and cold, and Biscuit gave a delighted little shiver. Maddy was checking her cat book and didn't notice when Biscuit edged a little further forward, and stuck her tongue in the bowl to lap up her leftover cereal. She got in a good few mouthfuls before Maddy spotted her.

"Biscuit! You shouldn't be eating that! Oh, Mum, look, she's got milk all over her whiskers!"

Biscuit settled back on to Maddy's lap, licking her whiskers happily. She liked her food better, but it was nice to have a change…

"Oh dear! I suppose a little bit won't have done her any harm. You'd finished, hadn't you? And yes, Donna gave us the vaccination certificate."

Mum looked in the folder she'd left on the countertop. "She had them done about three weeks ago."

Maddy checked the book again. "Then we need to take her to the vet soon! She's supposed to have the second vaccination three weeks after the first one. And then in another three weeks, she'll be allowed to go outside."

"Actually, yes, that's what Donna's put in this note. She said we should probably have Biscuit microchipped at the same time."

Maddy nodded. Her book mentioned that, too. The tiny microchip went under the skin on the kitten's neck, and it would have a special number on it, so that Biscuit could be easily identified by any vet if she got lost.

"I'll call the vet tomorrow, Maddy. They won't be open on a Sunday."

Maddy nodded. "That reminds me! Can I call Kate, Mum? I have to tell her about Biscuit!"

Luckily, the vet's had a cancelled appointment on Monday afternoon. Maddy wanted to get Biscuit's vaccinations done as soon as possible, so that she would be able to play with her in the garden. She knew that the little cat would love it. She was so adventurous inside the house. She kept climbing things, and she loved to tunnel under Maddy's duvet and then pop out at her.

For the trip to the vet's, Maddy put the cat carrier next to her on the back seat, and Biscuit peered out at her worriedly. She had only been in the cat carrier once, and that was to come to Maddy's house. Were they going back to her old home again? She did miss playing with her brothers and sisters, but Maddy was just as much fun to play with – and she didn't jump on top of her and try to chew her ears, like her biggest ginger brother had done. Biscuit definitely preferred Maddy's house. She let out a miserable wail as Maddy lifted the carrier out of the car – but then she realized that it wasn't her old home they'd come to after all.

The place smelled very odd; sharp and chemical to her sensitive nose.

But at the same time, it was slightly familiar. Had she been here before?

Maddy put the carrier down on the floor, and Biscuit sniffed suspiciously. There were other smells, too. A strange, strong, worrying smell. It smelled like a dog. A dog had visited her old home once, and she hadn't liked it. She shifted nervously inside her carrier. It was coming closer!

Biscuit gave a horrified squeak as a furry face loomed up in front of her carrier. The puppy peered in curiously and nudged the wire door with his nose.

The kitten bristled, her fur standing

on end and her tail fluffing up to twice its size. She hissed furiously at the dog. This was *her* carrier! She lashed her claws at his nose, but they scraped harmlessly down the wire.

"Barney, no!" his owner cried. "Oh, I'm so sorry, I hope he didn't frighten your kitten."

Maddy's mum laughed. "Actually, I think she tried to fight back; she's a determined little thing."

Maddy looked anxiously into Biscuit's carrier. "Are you all right? Sorry, Biscuit, I was helping Mum fill in the forms. I didn't see what was happening." Then she smiled with relief. Biscuit was sitting in the carrier with her tail wrapped smugly round her legs. She wasn't afraid of some silly dog!

Chapter Three

"She's going to miss me while I'm at school," Maddy said worriedly. She had her coat and her rucksack and her lunchbag – and a kitten sitting on her shoulder, sniffing with interest at the rucksack. "It's the first day I won't have been here to play with her."

"I'll be here though," her mum pointed out. Maddy's mum worked part-time at another school, but she didn't go in on Mondays or Fridays. "I'll play with her lots, Maddy, I promise. And your dad's working from home tomorrow. She'll gradually get used to being left. It'll be fine."

Maddy nodded doubtfully. She'd spent the whole holiday playing with Biscuit and fussing over her. Now she just couldn't imagine a whole day at school without seeing her. And without Kate…

"Come on, Maddy. We'd better go."

Maddy sighed and then carefully unhooked Biscuit's claws from her coat. She put her down gently and rubbed her ears. "Be good," she told her. "I'll be back soon."

Biscuit stared up at her. She didn't

understand what was happening, but she could tell from Maddy's voice that she wasn't happy. The kitten gave an uncertain little mew and patted at Maddy's leg with a paw, asking to be picked up again.

"Maddy, now," her mum said firmly, seeing that Maddy was close to tears. She shooed her out of the door, leaving Biscuit all alone in the house.

Biscuit sat by the front door for a little while, hoping that they'd come back, but she couldn't hear any footsteps heading up the path. She was very confused – she just didn't understand why Maddy had gone away. Eventually, she padded back into the kitchen. She had seen Maddy and her mum and dad use the back door, even though she wasn't allowed out of it yet. Perhaps they would come in that way?

She waited for what seemed like a very long time, but no one came in by that door, either. So she wandered through the house, mewing every so often. Where had they all gone? Were they ever coming back? She looked at the stairs for a while, but she still found them very difficult to climb. Maddy had carried her up there a couple of times, but it took her ages to manage a whole flight of stairs by herself.

Sadly, she trailed into the living room, and clawed her way up the purple throw that Maddy's mum had draped over the sofa. It already had quite a lot of little claw marks in it – Biscuit had quickly discovered that the back of the sofa was an interesting place to sit. She sat down, peering out of the window, hoping to see Maddy coming up the front path.

Instead, she saw a large gingery face staring back at her.

Biscuit was so surprised that she jumped backwards with a miaow of fright, and fell on to the seat of the sofa.

What was that? Another cat? In her garden? Biscuit had never been out in it, but she was quite certain that it was hers. She sat shivering on the sofa, not daring to climb up and look again. The other cat had been a lot bigger than she was. What if it was still there? At last, Biscuit scrabbled her way up the throw again, and peeped over the back of the sofa.

The big ginger cat had gone.

Biscuit was so relieved that she curled up on the back of the sofa, and went to sleep.

"She was fine, Maddy!" Mum said, as they walked home from school. "When I got home from dropping you off and doing the shopping, she was asleep on the back of the sofa. And then the rest of the day I fussed over her every so often, and she was perfectly all right."

Maddy nodded, looking relieved. "I wonder if she was watching for us coming home, and that's why she was on the back of the sofa."

"Maybe." Her mum laughed. "Actually, I think she's just nosy. She likes watching people go past. Anyway, how was school?"

Maddy could tell that her mum was trying not to sound worried about her. She shrugged. "OK."

"Who did you sit with?"

"Lucy. And Romany."

"And it was all right?"

"Mmm." Maddy didn't want to tell her mum that she'd felt miserable and lonely all day, and that even though Lucy and Romany had been nice, she'd hardly talked to them. She couldn't help thinking that they were Kate's friends, not hers, and they didn't really want to hang around with her. Luckily it had been netball club at lunch, so she hadn't had to mooch around on her own in the playground. But she didn't have a club every lunchtime. She sped up, hurrying home to see Biscuit.

"Oh, look, she's there, watching out for us!" Maddy beamed. She ran up the garden path, watching Biscuit leap off the back of the sofa. She could hear a little scuttle of paws, and then frantic mewing and a scrabbling noise as the kitten clawed at the door. As soon as her mum opened it, Maddy swept the kitten up to hug her.

School wasn't any easier the next day, or the day after that – but at least Maddy had Biscuit to cheer her up at home. And she was really looking forward to Saturday – the vet had said Biscuit could go out in the garden then, even though it wasn't quite three weeks since her vaccinations. He'd said it would be fine as long as she wasn't around any other cats.

Maddy didn't give Biscuit as much breakfast as usual on Saturday morning. And just in case Biscuit did wander too far, Maddy made sure she had a full bag of the kitten's favourite chicken-flavour treats.

Biscuit was still staring suspiciously at her food bowl, wondering why breakfast hadn't seemed to take as long to gobble down as usual, when she realized that the back door was wide open. She'd seen it open before, of course, but only when someone was holding her tightly, and even then they always whipped it shut before she could wriggle free and go investigating. She crept over to it, keeping low to the ground, expecting any minute that Maddy or her mum would catch her.

But Maddy was outside! She was standing by the door, calling her! Biscuit hurried so fast out of the door, she almost tripped over the step. She shook herself crossly and pattered down the path to where Maddy was.

There were so many smells! She sniffed curiously at the grass, and patted it with one paw. It was cool and damp, and taller than she was!

"Have you got the treats?" Her mum appeared in the doorway. "In case Biscuit goes running off. She could get under the fence if she really tried, remember."

Maddy waved the foil packet. "It's OK. Oh, look, Mum! She's seen a butterfly!"

The orange butterfly was swooping carelessly past Biscuit's nose, and she watched it in amazement. Maddy had dangled pieces of string for her, and feathery toys, but she had never seen anything like this. She reached out her paw and tried to bat at the butterfly, and then tried again with the other paw, but it flew behind her, and she almost fell over trying to chase after it.

"You can't have it, Biscuit," Maddy

laughed. "I don't think butterflies are very good for you. And they're all legs and wings; I bet they don't taste nice."

Biscuit stared after the butterfly, which was flittering over the fence to next door's garden. She thought it looked delicious. But there was no way she could get over the high fence to follow it.

Chapter Four

Maddy and Biscuit spent so much time playing in the garden that on Friday evening, Maddy's dad came home with a surprise. He put the big box he was carrying down in front of Biscuit's cat basket with a flourish.

"What is it?" Maddy asked, peering round to see the front of the box. Biscuit blinked at it sleepily. She was worn out from racing round the garden with Maddy after she had got back from school.

"Oh, a cat flap! Thanks, Dad!"

"We can put it in tomorrow. It's over three weeks since Biscuit had her vaccinations now, so we can let her out on her own."

Maddy nodded. "I suppose so. But she's still not quite fourteen weeks old. She's only little."

"I think cats like to explore though," Dad pointed out. "She'll be able to climb trees. Chase more butterflies…"

Biscuit suddenly perked up, bouncing up in her basket and staring at him, ears pricked. Dad laughed. "You see!"

Maddy had been worried that Biscuit might find the cat flap hard to work, or that she just might not like it – Kate had told her that Ben had taken ages to get used to his. He preferred to have someone open the back door for him. But as soon as Biscuit understood what the cat flap did, she took to it immediately. She spent most of Saturday afternoon popping in and out of it, coming back into the kitchen every five minutes to make sure that Maddy was still there.

Maddy had been a bit anxious that Biscuit might try going into one of the next-door gardens, but even though she'd sniffed at the holes under the fence, she didn't seem to want to crawl through them. There was plenty in Maddy's garden to keep her busy.

Maddy was doing her homework at the kitchen table on Sunday morning, with Biscuit curled on her lap. Her science worksheet seemed to be taking ages. It was probably because she kept thinking about her science lesson on Friday. She'd had to pair up with Sara, a girl she didn't really like, and Sara had kept on making mean little comments throughout the lesson. So now every time she tried to write about the differences between solids and liquids, she just started thinking about how much she missed having Kate to work with. Kate would have said something really funny about Sara, Maddy was sure.

At least she'd seen Becky, one of the girls who sat on the table behind her, making faces at Sara. She'd rolled her eyes at Maddy in an "Ignore her!" sort of way, and Maddy had smiled back.

Now Biscuit yawned and jumped lazily off Maddy's lap, making for her cat flap. She was bored with sitting still, and Maddy didn't seem to want to play. Biscuit had tried chasing her coloured pencils across the table, but Maddy had put them away instead of rolling the pencils for her to chase.

The garden was full of interesting smells, and some bees were buzzing around the lavender bushes. Biscuit watched them, fascinated, her tail tip twitching. She was watching so closely that she didn't see Tiger and Tom sneaking under next door's fence. It wasn't until the two big ginger cats were right behind her that Biscuit heard them creeping through the grass, and whirled round. She was sure it was one of these cats who'd been staring in at her through the window.

The ginger cats had their ears laid back as they snuck towards her. Biscuit backed away from them into the lavender bush. She didn't quite understand what was happening, but she knew the two cats weren't friendly. Her tail bushed out, and she darted a nervous glance towards the door. Could she make a run for her cat flap? But one of the big ginger cats, the one with the torn ear, was between her and the house, his tail swishing from side to side.

Tiger, the one with the darker stripes, was almost nose to nose with her now, hissing and staring. Biscuit was practically squashed into the lavender bush – she couldn't retreat any further.

Tiger cuffed her round the head with one enormous paw, sending her rolling, and Biscuit wailed miserably. What was she supposed to do? Why were they attacking her?

Inside the house, Maddy was still gloomily eyeing her homework. She glanced up as her mum came into the kitchen, looking confused.

"Maddy, can you hear a strange noise? It almost sounds like a baby crying. A sort of howling."

Maddy yelped and suddenly pushed her chair away from the table, racing for the back door. She hadn't been paying attention to the noise, but now she was sure it was Biscuit.

She flung open the door, and Tom jumped round, hissing at her, but Tiger and Biscuit hardly seemed to notice. They were in the middle of the lawn now, and Tiger was about three times the size of Biscuit with all his ginger fur fluffed up. They were making strange wowling noises still, circling round each other. As Maddy watched, Tiger leaped on Biscuit again, and the two cats seemed to roll over and over, twisting and scratching.

"Stop it!" Maddy yelled. She raced over to them, shoving at Tiger, ignoring the hissing and scratching at her hands. She snatched Biscuit up, and yelled at Tiger and Tom, sending them scuttling away under the fence.

"Maddy, are you all right?" Her mum came running out. "It all happened so quickly, I didn't realize what was going on. Is Biscuit hurt?"

"I don't think so, but she's shaking." Maddy carried the kitten inside. "Those horrible cats!"

Her mum sighed. "I suppose they're used to coming into our garden. They think Biscuit's in their territory."

"Well, she isn't!" Maddy snapped. "It's our garden and she's our cat!"

"Yes, we know that, but I bet the cats don't. Give her to me, you need to run your hands under the tap. They must hurt, you're all scratched!"

Reluctantly, Maddy handed Biscuit over to her mum.

"She's so scared," Maddy said, her

voice shaking as she washed her hands. "Tiger's so much bigger than she is. He could have really hurt her." Then she laughed a little. "I saw Biscuit scratch his nose, though, before he ran off."

"Did they go under the fence?" her mum asked. "Is there a hole we could block up?"

Maddy dried her scratched hands and made for the door. "I'll go and see."

Biscuit gave a worried little mew as she saw Maddy opening the door, and Maddy stopped to stroke her. "Don't worry. I'm not going to let those ginger bullies anywhere near you."

She hurried out into the garden, checking the fence. There were holes all the way along – not huge ones, but big enough for a cat to squeeze through.

It was going to be difficult to block them all up. And the fence wasn't that high, either. She was pretty sure that Tiger and Tom could climb it without too much effort.

"What are you doing?" someone asked in a sneery sort of voice.

Maddy straightened up from the flower bed. It was her next-door neighbour Josh, who owned Tiger and Tom. He was a couple of years older than she was and went to secondary school, so usually Maddy was too shy to say much to him. But not today.

"I'm looking at the fence! Your cats just came into my garden and beat up my kitten!" she snapped at him.

Josh shrugged. "Sorry. But cats fight. It's what they do."

"Don't you care? She's terrified!"

"There isn't anything I can do, cats chase each other and they fight. There's loads of cats round here. Your kitten's going to get into fights, Maddy, stop being such a girl."

"OH!" Maddy huffed, and she stomped back inside. Biscuit was not going to fight, because Maddy wasn't going to let any other cats hurt her. She didn't care how scratched *she* got.

But as she shut the kitchen door, slamming it hard enough to set the cat flap swinging, Maddy had a sudden, awful thought.

She could protect Biscuit now, but what about tomorrow, when she went back to school?

"Perhaps we shouldn't have got a cat flap..." Maddy said worriedly.

Her dad scratched his head thoughtfully. He'd been out running when Biscuit got into the fight, and had missed the whole thing. "I can't exactly put that chunk of door back.

Anyway, Biscuit's getting bigger all the time. She won't be such easy pickings for those two next door soon."

"I don't think Biscuit's ever going to be as big as they are," Maddy said. "But it's good for her to be able to go out. She loves being in the garden! Or she did, anyway," she added sadly.

Biscuit hadn't been outside again since the fight that morning. She'd retreated into the dining room. There was a lovely patch of warm sun coming through the glass doors at the back of the room. Biscuit lay in it, feeling the soft warmth on her fur. It made her feel better – not so jumpy and scared.

She stretched out on the carpet lazily and gazed out of the big window through half-open eyes, hoping to spot some butterflies.

Instead, the next time she blinked, Tiger and Tom were there. In her garden, staring at her, just on the other side of the window.

Biscuit's tail fluffed up and she hissed in panic. For a moment, she forgot that there was glass there and they couldn't reach her through it. She was sure that Tiger was about to knock her over again. She raced out to the kitchen and Maddy, mewing in fright.

"Oh! They're back in the garden!" Maddy picked Biscuit up, cuddling her.

Dad quickly filled up a glass that was by the sink and headed out into the garden. But he came back shaking his head. "I was going to splash them –

cats don't like getting wet – but they'd gone already."

"If they keep doing this, Biscuit's going to be frightened all the time," Maddy said anxiously. "It's so unfair."

She was still worrying when she went to bed that night. She'd left the kitten snoozing in her basket in the kitchen, after putting some of Biscuit's favourite chicken crunchies in her bowl, in case she woke up needing a midnight snack.

It took Maddy ages to get to sleep. She tossed and turned, thinking about Tiger and Tom, and then about school tomorrow and how lonely it was going to be. Somehow it all got wound up into her dreams when she finally fell asleep, so that she was sitting doing numeracy with Tiger and Tom (in school uniform) on either side of her. Tiger was just telling her that she was stupid and she'd got her multiplication wrong, when Tom started wowling in her ear. Maddy twitched, turned over – and woke up. That wasn't in her dream – the sound was coming from downstairs!

She flung herself out of bed and dashed down the stairs. The noise was louder now and it was coming from the kitchen. Maddy couldn't understand – it sounded like more than one cat, but only Biscuit was meant to be in there. She shoved open the door, and saw Tiger and Tom by Biscuit's food bowl, gobbling down the chicken crunchies she'd left out.

"Go away!" Maddy yelled. "Out! Bad cats!" Tiger and Tom hissed at her, but hightailed it out of the cat flap. The cat flap – of course. That's how they'd got into Maddy's kitchen!

"What on earth…?" Dad appeared in the kitchen doorway, looking sleepy.

"The cats from next door! They came in through the cat flap, Dad; they were eating Biscuit's food!" Maddy crouched down by Biscuit's bed. She looked terrified, and as Maddy gently picked her up, she could feel how tense the kitten was, as though she was ready to leap out of Maddy's arm and run away at any moment. Her whiskers were twitching, and her little face seemed all frightened eyes.

Mum had been worried that Biscuit might end up making a mess in Maddy's room if she slept upstairs, but Maddy couldn't bear the thought of leaving her on her own.

"Dad, please can I take Biscuit upstairs to sleep with me?" she begged. "I know Mum said she should stay in the kitchen, but she's so scared."

Dad sighed. "I suppose she is very well house-trained now. And she's got pretty good at the stairs, hasn't she?

She'll be all right to come down if she needs her litter tray. I'm going to put a chair in front of the cat flap, in case Tiger and Tom come back."

Maddy nodded. Biscuit was relaxing into her arms a little now, but she was still looking around nervously. Maddy hurried upstairs and fluffed up her duvet into a cosy kitten nest at the end of the bed. It didn't leave much duvet for her, but she didn't mind.

Biscuit stepped cautiously into the warm nest and padded at it with her paws. Maddy was here. She was safe. Tiger and Tom wouldn't be able to come upstairs, she was sure. And if they did, Maddy would chase them away.

Maddy slid into bed and sighed. She'd wanted Biscuit to sleep on her bed ever since she'd got her, but she wished it hadn't happened like this.

Maddy was just falling asleep again when she felt determined little paws padding up her tummy, and a soft wisp of fur brushed across her cheek as Biscuit curled up next to her on the pillow. Maddy giggled. Biscuit's tail was lying across her neck and it tickled.

"We'll sort those horrible cats out," she told Biscuit sleepily. "It'll be OK."

Chapter Five

"Time to get up!" Maddy's mum pulled open the bedroom curtains.

"Mmmm. Oh!" Maddy suddenly remembered that Biscuit was upstairs with her, although she was no longer asleep on her pillow.

"Your dad told me he'd let you bring Biscuit up here. I suppose it isn't doing any harm, as long as you make sure she doesn't get shut in. We don't want her weeing on your bedroom carpet!" She looked around. "Where is she? Has she gone downstairs already?"

Maddy sat up. "She was sleeping next to me."

"She's here!" Her mum was crouching down, peering under the bed. "It's all right, Biscuit, I'm not scary. Oh dear, Maddy, she looks very nervous."

"Maybe she heard you coming in and thought it was Tiger and Tom again." Maddy hopped out of bed to look underneath.

Biscuit was squeezed as far back as she could go, pressed against the wall. Maddy could see her whiskers trembling. "Biscuit! Come on, it's OK."

Very slowly, Biscuit crept out and let Maddy pick her up. But she flinched when Maddy's mum tried to stroke her.

"She's usually so friendly," Maddy's mum said sadly. "Perhaps she'll feel better after some food."

"I hope so." Maddy carried Biscuit downstairs with her once she'd got dressed. She could feel Biscuit tensing up as they came down the hall into the kitchen. She was practically clinging on to Maddy's cardigan, and she didn't seem very interested in eating even when Maddy filled up her bowl.

"Don't worry, I'll keep an eye on her while you're at school," Mum said. "How are things going, anyway?"

Maddy shrugged.

"I know you're missing Kate, but I'm sure there are lots of other people in your class that you could chat to," her mum said persuasively.

But none of them are as nice as Kate, Maddy thought. *And none of them want to chat to me. It just isn't that easy...*

"It's a month till Sports Day," Mrs Melling, Maddy's teacher explained, as she led everyone out on to the school field. "So we're going to be doing some athletics – running, hurdles, relay races, that sort of thing."

Several people sighed grumpily, but Maddy smiled. She loved to run. And she was pretty good at it, too. The sun was shining, and she could feel it on her hair and her arms. She'd been worrying about Biscuit all morning, even though Dad had left the cat flap blocked up, in case Tiger and Tom tried to get in again. Maddy knew Biscuit should be fine, but she couldn't stop thinking about her, and how frightened she'd been. Hopefully some running would shake off the jittery, miserable feeling inside her.

The school field had a big oval track painted on to the grass, and after they'd warmed up, Mrs Melling divided them into groups to run heats. Maddy won her first heat easily – none of the others were really trying – but she was surprised when she beat a couple of boys in the next race. Some of the girls even started cheering for her at the end.

"Well done! You're so quick!" Becky came over and patted her on the back.

Maddy laughed, a little nervously. She'd always liked Becky, but she was really popular and had lots of friends. She was nice to Maddy, but they'd never hung around together much.

"Beat Joe in this last race, please!" Becky begged. "He's so full of himself, look at him!"

Joe was talking to a couple of other boys and doing show-off stretches. He obviously thought he was bound to win.

"OK." Maddy grinned. She wasn't tired at all. As they lined up for the last race she bounced on her toes, staring at the finish line. As soon as Mrs Melling blew her whistle, she shot away, sprinting as fast as she could, and crossed the finish line a whisker ahead of Joe.

"Yay! Maddy wins!" She could hear Becky yelling above all the others. It felt fantastic.

With Becky and the others hugging her and telling her she was a star, it was easy to laugh off Joe growling about girls always cheating. And Becky's table in class was behind hers, so Maddy could see Becky grinning at her every so often as they did their literacy after PE. It was the best time she'd had in school all term. She couldn't wait to tell her mum and dad about it. They kept asking how school was going – it would be nice to be able to say she'd had a fun day.

"How was Biscuit?" Maddy asked hopefully, as she rushed up to her mum after school.

Mum made a face. "She's been scratching the sofa! I had to shut her out of the living room."

"Oh..." Maddy frowned. Biscuit had never done that before. She hoped Mum hadn't been too cross with her.

When they got home, Maddy put her bags down, expecting the kitten to bounce up to her, wanting to play, like she usually did. But Biscuit didn't come running.

"Biscuit!" Maddy looked round anxiously.

"Try upstairs," her mum suggested. "She seems to like it there now."

Maddy ran up the stairs and into her room. She couldn't see Biscuit, but she had a horrible feeling she knew where she was. She knelt down, looking under the bed, and sighed. She was right. Biscuit was curled up in the corner again, 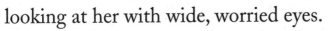 looking at her with wide, worried eyes.

"Oh, Biscuit..." Maddy whispered. "It's all right, sweetie, come on out..."

"I don't think we can keep the cat flap blocked up like that," Dad said, looking down at his ice cream thoughtfully. "Biscuit needs to be able to go out."

"But she doesn't want to," Maddy explained. "She's scared."

"It isn't good to keep her in – she should be out sharpening her claws on trees, not the sofa," Mum sighed.

"And it would be nice not to have to keep cleaning out the litter tray!"

"I'll do it," Maddy said quickly. "I don't mind. She's too frightened to go in the garden."

She licked her ice-cream spoon, but she wasn't really hungry any more. She could feel Mum and Dad both looking at her. And she was pretty sure they thought she was fussing too much.

"I think Biscuit might just need to toughen up a bit," Dad said gently.

"She's definitely getting bigger," Mum pointed out. "She'll be as big as Tiger and Tom soon."

"I bet she won't," Maddy said. "And however big she is, there's still only one of her. Tiger and Tom work as a team, Mum! Like wrestlers!"

Her mum frowned, and glanced meaningfully at her dad. Maddy knew what that look meant. They thought she was fussing about Biscuit because of school. Because she was feeling nervous and worried too. Mum and Dad reckoned Maddy needed to toughen up a bit, and make some new friends.

"I'll go and look on the net for some ideas," she said quickly, wanting to get away before they started asking about school again, and if there was anyone she wanted to invite to tea. *But maybe I could ask Becky over?* she thought for a second, and then crushed the idea firmly. Becky was far too popular to want to hang around with her.

"You want to do what?" Josh made a snorting noise.

"A timeshare…" Maddy repeated, wriggling to keep her elbows on top of the fence. She was standing on a bucket to see over the fence and it was a bit wobbly. "You keep Tiger and Tom in some of the time, so Biscuit can go out without them scaring her."

After tea, she'd turned on the computer to search her favourite pet advice websites, and found an email waiting for her from Kate. Maddy had sent her a message a couple of days ago, asking if she had any advice. The timeshare idea was something Kate had read about once, and it sounded perfect.

Maddy took a deep breath. She didn't like talking to Josh; he always made her feel stupid. But she had to. "Please can you think about it? Biscuit's getting really twitchy and nervous. It wouldn't have to be long. Maybe only for an hour a day? Just until she's bigger and she can stand up for herself."

Josh shrugged. "How am I supposed to keep them in? Tiger and Tom have a cat flap. They go in and out whenever they want to."

"But couldn't you—" Maddy began.

"I've got football, I need to go," Josh interrupted. And he disappeared through his back door, leaving Maddy peering over the fence after him.

Maddy sighed. The timeshare had seemed like such a good idea. Except that stupid Josh couldn't be bothered!

She trailed back into the kitchen, and found Biscuit sitting on one of the chairs, staring anxiously at the cat flap – Maddy had moved the chair blocking it so she could get out.

"We'll have to think of something else," she told Biscuit, tickling her under the chin.

Biscuit rubbed her head against Maddy's hand and purred.

She really trusts me, Maddy thought. *I have to sort this out somehow…*

Chapter Six

Biscuit didn't go out on her own at all for the rest of the week. Maddy took her out into the garden a few times, as she was pretty sure Tiger and Tom wouldn't come into the garden if she was there. But as soon as she put Biscuit down, the little tortoiseshell would race for her cat flap. And even when she was inside, she spent most of her time hiding under Maddy's bed. She even weed on the floor a couple of times, which made Mum cross.

"I know it isn't her fault, Maddy," Mum told her on Friday morning, as she scrubbed at the landing carpet. "But the smell is horrible!"

"You don't want us to give her back to Donna, do you?" Maddy asked anxiously.

Mum shook her head. "No... But we need to sort this out. Anyway, we'd better get off to school now."

Biscuit watched them from under the bathroom towel rail. She liked it there. It was warm and dark, and the bathroom didn't have any windows she could see other cats from. She hadn't gone downstairs to eat yet. She wasn't sure she was brave enough. What if Tiger and Tom came back into the kitchen again?

As the front door banged behind Maddy, Biscuit crept out to the top of the stairs. She was so hungry, she would have to risk the kitchen. She hurried down the stairs and peered round the kitchen door. No sign of any strange cats. Gratefully, she hurried in, and started to gulp down her food, stopping every few seconds to glance around worriedly.

About halfway through her bowl, she began to relax a little, and slowed down enough to enjoy the food.

Then the front door banged and she leaped away from the bowl in fright. Was it Tiger and Tom again?

Panicking, Biscuit shot into the corner of the kitchen, trying to hide. She was so frightened that she weed all over the floor.

"Oh, no! Biscuit!" Maddy's mum said crossly, as she got back and saw the mess. "What on earth did you do that for? It's only me." She went to the cupboard under the sink to get some spray and a cloth. "Go on, shoo. I've got to wipe it up now." She flapped the cloth at Biscuit grumpily.

Biscuit was so jittery that the flash of the white cloth scared her, and she shot out of the cat flap to get away from it. Maddy's mum had gone to fetch the mop, and she didn't notice that the kitten had gone.

Biscuit sat on the back step, staring

around the garden. She hadn't been outside for a week, and there were so many tempting smells. And there were bees, buzzing about by the lavender bushes. And butterflies… Cautiously, she padded out on to the lawn, shivering deliciously as the sun hit her fur.

She didn't even see Tiger before he leaped out from under the fence, and spat at her. She turned to race for the cat flap, but he chased her, knocking her sideways and clawing her ear. Biscuit looked around for Tom, wondering if he was about to jump out at her too, but Tiger seemed to be on his own for once. Not that it mattered – he was still more than twice as big as she was and horribly fierce. Biscuit mewed with fright as Tiger pounced at her again. She was never going to be able to get away. Unless… She tried to scratch him, shooting out a sharp-clawed paw, and he retreated a little, hissing. It gave her time to think.

If she couldn't beat him running, perhaps she could go up over the fence? Anything was worth a try. She jumped at Tiger suddenly, clawing him again, and then raced past him, heading for the fence. She scrambled up it, scrabbling and fighting for the top. Then she perched there, wobbling, and looked down at Tiger, who stared back up at her.

Biscuit gave a frightened little squeak, and jumped off the other side of the fence…

"Mum, where's Biscuit? I thought she'd be under my bed, but I can't find her anywhere. I've looked in all the places she usually goes."

Mum frowned. "I haven't actually seen her much today. She weed on the kitchen floor this morning… But I'm not sure when I saw her after that. I had to go and do some shopping, and then I came straight back from town to pick you up."

Maddy looked at Biscuit's bed, as though she might suddenly appear from underneath it. Then she noticed the cat flap. "Oh! You moved the chair!"

"I had to," Mum said grimly. "I was wiping up cat wee round it. I see what you mean though, she might have gone out. But that's good, Maddy! We want her to start going outside again."

"Not if those two thugs from next door are around," Maddy muttered. "I'm going to check outside for her."

But there was no sign of Biscuit in the garden either, even after Maddy called and called.

"Can't you see her?" her mum asked, leaning out of the kitchen door. She was looking slightly worried now too.

350

"No, and we normally feed her about now."

"I'll look upstairs again, perhaps she got shut in somewhere," Mum said.

Maddy knew she'd already checked everywhere, but she nodded anyway. "Biscuit! Biscuit!" she called again.

"Have you lost your kitten?"

Maddy jumped. She hadn't realized Josh was out in his garden. "Yes, you haven't seen her, have you?"

"Nope."

Maddy sighed. "Could you look out for her? Please?"

"Yeah, all right." But he didn't sound very bothered, Maddy thought.

She ran back inside. "Mum, do you think we should go and look for her? Oh, but we can't!"

"Why not?" Her mum looked confused.

"If your cat gets lost, it's best to leave someone they know in the house – otherwise they might not think it's their home if they come back. My book said so."

"Really? OK, well, if she's not back when Dad gets home, you and I can go and look for her then."

The hour before Maddy's dad got home seemed to crawl past. Maddy kept searching the same places over and over again, just in case she'd somehow missed Biscuit the first five or six times she'd checked.

As soon as she saw her dad at the gate, Maddy was out of the front door and running down the path.

"Biscuit's lost! We're going to look for her, you have to stay here!" she gasped.

Her dad stared at her, and then at Mum, dashing down the path after her.

Maddy's mum looked at him worriedly. "I said we'd go and look round the streets. I don't think she could have gone far."

Maddy was already hurrying down the road, peering under the parked cars. "Come on, Mum!" she called.

Biscuit peered miserably out at the strange garden. As she'd jumped off the fence, she'd been trying to look behind her at the same time, and she'd landed badly, jarring one of her front paws.

It hurt, and so did the scratches. But she'd kept going, desperate to get as far away from Tiger as she could. She'd crawled under fence after fence, hurrying on and on, until at last she felt as if she might be safe. She'd smelled several other cats and even seen a couple, but none of them had chased her yet.

Eventually she'd stopped to rest behind a garden shed. She didn't feel like she could go any further, her paw hurt so much. She'd huddled there for the rest of the day, unsure what to do. She couldn't go home, could she? Tiger would chase her again. She'd have to wait until she was sure Maddy was back, then it would be safe.

They searched for ages. Maddy kept looking at the road and hoping that Biscuit hadn't been so scared she'd run out in front of a car. *I should have taken more care of her. I ought to have made Josh do something about Tiger and Tom,* she kept thinking. *When I find Biscuit, I'm going to tell him!*

They were halfway down the next road and Maddy was hanging over a garden wall staring into some tall flowers, when a surprised voice said, "What are you doing?"

Maddy jumped. She hadn't even

noticed anyone approach. Becky from school was standing behind her, while her mum locked up the car. She was wearing a cardigan over ballet clothes, and peering over the wall to see what Maddy was looking at.

"Oh! Hi, Becky. I'm looking for my kitten." Maddy gulped and swallowed. "She's lost..." It was so horrible to say it.

"Oh no! The cute little tortoiseshell one? You've got her photo in your locker, haven't you?"

Maddy nodded. She was surprised Becky had noticed.

"Want me to help look? Can I, Mum? We were just coming back from ballet," Becky explained. "This is our house. I didn't know you lived so close to us."

Maddy went red. "Sorry about looking in your garden," she said to Becky's mum.

"Don't worry," she replied with a smile. "You can help Maddy look up and down our road, Becky. But only until it's dark – you've probably got another half an hour, that's all."

Maddy looked around anxiously. Biscuit had never even been out at night! She hated the thought of her being all alone and scared in the dark.

The two girls went on up the road, calling for Biscuit, and Becky's mum joined in too, asking their neighbours if they'd seen a kitten. But no one had.

"We have to stop, it's too dark," Maddy's mum said eventually.

"We can't!" Maddy said pleadingly.

"I'll come and help you look first thing tomorrow," Becky told her, giving her a hug. "Don't worry. We'll find her."

At last, as it was starting to get dark, Biscuit decided she could leave her hiding place. Maddy must be home by now. As long as she could get back in through her cat flap before Tiger spotted her, she would be safe.

She crawled out of the dark space behind the shed, wincing as she tried to put her weight on the hurt paw. It seemed to be getting worse. She limped across the garden, and squeezed under the fence, only to see a pair of glinting amber eyes, glaring at her from under a bush. She backed away nervously. Her first thought was that it was Tiger, but it didn't smell like him. It was a strange smell – strong and fierce. And the creature it belonged to was big…

The fox darted forward, and snapped at her, his teeth huge and yellow.

Biscuit ran blindly. She didn't know

where she was going – just away. She darted down the side passage, under a gate and out on to the pavement, where she stopped and glanced quickly behind her. The fox wasn't following. But now she had even less idea where she was, and her paw was throbbing after her panicked dash. She limped on, hobbling down the kerb. She needed to rest, and there was a garden on the other side of the road that looked like a good hiding place, overgrown, with bushes spilling over a low fence. Biscuit set off across the road, not understanding the low growl of the car turning the corner.

She was halfway across when she noticed it – the huge machine that seemed to be towering over her, its

lights dazzling her.
The car braked
sharply, its tyres
squealing on
the tarmac.
Biscuit wailed
as she dived forward out of the way, her
injured paw collapsing underneath her,
so that she half-dragged herself across
the road. She struggled through the gate
of the overgrown garden and flung
herself down under the dark bushes,
her breath coming in terrified gasps.
She was so tired, and everything seemed
to hurt.

Biscuit lay there, gazing into the dark
night. She had no idea where she was,
or how to get back to Maddy. What
was she going to do?

Chapter Seven

Becky's mum dropped her round first thing on Saturday morning. "It's not too early, is it?" Becky asked. "Mum said it might be, but I told her you'd want to get looking straight away."

Maddy half-smiled. "I've been up for ages. I'm just waiting for Dad. It's really nice of you to come."

Becky shook her head. "I said

I would! I want to help you find her."

Maddy's dad appeared behind her. "Ready, girls?"

As they came out of the gate, Tiger and Tom prowled down Josh's front path and leaped on to the wall, staring at them with round green eyes.

Maddy clenched her fists. "Look at them! They're so mean!"

"Are they the ones who scared Biscuit?" Becky asked. Maddy had told her how frightened Biscuit had been.

Maddy nodded. "They're horrible."

Becky pushed open Josh's gate, glaring at the ginger cats. "Come on! Don't you think we should make Josh help us look?"

"I suppose so," Maddy faltered. She shook herself. "Yes, he should."

"Come on then," said Maddy's dad.

Maddy stomped up the path and rang the doorbell hard. She was a bit shocked when Josh's dad answered the front door. She'd been expecting Josh.

"Um… We wondered…"

"Your cats chased her kitten away," Becky put in, over Maddy's shoulder.

Maddy's dad nodded. "She's lost, I'm afraid. We haven't seen her since yesterday morning."

Josh's dad looked worried. "Josh did say something about Tiger and Tom having a fight with a new cat…"

Maddy nodded. "We think they had another fight, and she ran off."

"Oh dear. Look, Josh has got to get to his football match, but can we come and help you look afterwards?"

"Thanks," Maddy told him, and the girls set off to search again.

Biscuit twitched and wriggled in her sleep, then woke up with a jolt, her fur all on end. She stared around the thick bushes, searching for the strange creature that had been chasing her. It had been even bigger than Tiger and Tom. But the gloomy space under the branches was empty – just her and a few beetles. She'd only been dreaming.

She peered out from under the bushes into the overgrown garden, her whiskers twitching.

The house had been abandoned, and the garden was covered in brambles and weeds. Biscuit shivered in the early morning chill. She was stiff all over. She wasn't used to sleeping outside. She hadn't meant to, either, she'd been planning to hurry home to Maddy. But the car had frightened her so much, she'd crawled into this safe little hole and fallen into an exhausted sleep.

Now she had to get home to Maddy. And Maddy would feed her too. She was so hungry, it seemed ages since she'd last had anything to eat.

Biscuit stood up, ready to creep out of her hiding place, but then she collapsed, mewing with pain as her paw seemed to double up underneath her. She'd forgotten. She tried again, putting her weight on her other front paw, but she could hardly move. She was so stiff, and her injured paw was dragging painfully as she limped through the damp grass. She had to stop and rest every few steps, and her paw was hurting more and more now. Finally, Biscuit sank down at the edge of the weedy gravel path. She couldn't go any further for a while. She was frozen, her fur was soaked through from the dew, and she was aching all over and so very tired.

How was she ever going to get home?

"If we don't find her soon, maybe we ought to make a poster?" Becky said. They'd searched all down Maddy's road again, and gone round the park, and the maze of little streets between the park and school. Now they were going back down Becky's road.

Maddy swallowed. "Yes," she whispered. It made sense. They'd been searching all morning. But it seemed like admitting that Biscuit was properly lost. Lost Cat posters always made her so sad. She couldn't imagine seeing Biscuit's photo stuck up on all the lamp posts.

"Let's keep calling her for a bit longer," she whispered. She rubbed her eyes to wipe away the tears, then shouted, "Biscuit! Biscuit!"

Curled up by the garden path, Biscuit was startled out of her cold half-sleep. That was Maddy, she was sure! She struggled to get up, but she couldn't stand on her hurt leg at all now. What if Maddy didn't see her? The garden was so overgrown, Maddy might easily miss her. Biscuit wailed desperately, a long heartbroken meow.

On the other side of the road, Maddy stopped suddenly, almost bumping into Becky. "Did you hear that?"

"Yes! Do you think it was Biscuit?"

Maddy's dad came running up the road. "Maddy, I think I heard—"

"I know! We did too! Come on!" Grabbing Becky by the hand, she hurried across the road. "It sounds like Biscuit's in that tangly old garden!"

Becky nodded. "I think you're right. No one lives in that house any more, it's really quiet. And spooky. I don't like walking past it. But it would be a good place to hide if she was scared."

Biscuit could hear Maddy getting closer. She called again, mewing desperately, and scrabbled her way down the path, dragging her useless leg.

"She's here!" Maddy flung the gate open. "Oh, Biscuit, you're hurt! She can't walk, Dad."

"Has she been hit by a car?" Becky asked anxiously.

Maddy picked up Biscuit, as gently

as she could. "I'm not sure. Her paw's hanging a bit funny, but it's not bleeding. She's scratched, though, all round her ears and nose. I knew Tiger and Tom had been after her again!"

"We'd better get her looked over by the vet," said Dad, taking out his phone.

Biscuit lay in Maddy's arms, purring faintly. Maddy had found her. She should have known. She rubbed her chin lovingly against Maddy's jumper. She wasn't leaving her, ever again.

Chapter Eight

"Is she going to be all right?" Maddy asked, exchanging an anxious look with Becky. Becky had begged to be allowed to come to the vet; she was desperate to know if Biscuit was going to be OK.

The vet nodded slowly. "I think she's just torn a muscle in her leg. She probably jumped and landed badly. She just needs to rest it. And I'll clean up these scratches and give her an injection of antibiotics, just in case. You said she's had trouble with the neighbour's cats? Looks like she's had a hard time."

Maddy nodded. "She won't go outside, she's so scared. They even came in through her cat flap. I think that was the worst thing. I'm not sure she feels safe even inside the house now."

The vet glanced at his computer screen. "She is microchipped, isn't she?"

"Yes, we had it done with her vaccinations," Dad said. "Why?"

"There's a new kind of cat flap you can get – it's a bit expensive, but it works off the microchip. So only your cat will be able to use it, you see."

Maddy looked up at Dad hopefully. "Can I have one of those for my birthday, just a bit early? Please?"

Dad was grinning. "Two months early? We might be able to stretch to it."

"You can program it, as well, so you can keep Biscuit in at night, if you like," the vet added.

Maddy nodded. "Then if Josh and his dad agree to keep Tiger and Tom in some of the time, we could tell the cat flap only to let Biscuit out when we know they're inside!"

"Was it two tomcats who were fighting her?" the vet asked. "Are they neutered? Boy cats can be rough, if they haven't been. It might be worth suggesting to their owner that he gets them done. I'll give you a leaflet."

"We'll talk to Josh's dad, Maddy," Dad promised.

As Dad drove back home, Maddy cradled Biscuit in her lap. They'd gone off to the vet's in such a rush, they hadn't had time to put her in her travel crate.

"I'll drop you two off, and then I'll go and see if that big pet shop by the supermarket has those special cat flaps," Dad said, as he pulled in.

"Look, there's Josh and his dad!" Maddy got out, carrying Biscuit.

"You found her!" Josh's dad hurried forward. "Is she OK?"

"She's hurt her paw and we had to take her to the vet," Maddy explained.

"She's really scratched, too…" Josh's dad peered at Biscuit's nose. "Was that our two?"

Maddy nodded. "I think so. Um, are Tiger and Tom neutered? The vet said maybe that would help. He gave us a leaflet."

Becky pushed the leaflet into Josh's dad's hand. "Probably not," he said. "We didn't have them done – they were strays, you see. They turned up at work, about three years ago now, and I brought them home. They were only tiny – about the size of your little one."

"Ohh…" Somehow, knowing that Tiger and Tom had been stray kittens made Maddy feel less cross with them. And Josh and his dad. It wasn't as if they'd asked to be cat owners, and they'd never realized how important it was to have the cats neutered.

"We can try and keep them in sometimes as well, like you said," Josh put in suddenly.

"That would be brilliant," Maddy said gratefully. She brushed her cheek lightly over Biscuit's soft furry head. It was all going to be OK... She should ring Kate to tell her what had happened, she thought suddenly, smiling. It was a nice thought. It didn't make her feel teary, like it would have done a couple of days ago. She missed Kate loads, still. But it wasn't as bad any more, somehow...

"I suppose I'd better get home," Becky said, as they reached Maddy's.

"Would your mum let you stay for a bit?" Maddy asked hopefully.

"That's OK, isn't it?" she added to her mum, who had come to the garden gate and was looking anxiously at Biscuit. "It's good news, Mum, the vet says she's probably just torn a muscle."

"Of course you can stay, after all your help. Ring your mum, Becky. Is she really all right?" Maddy's mum stroked Biscuit gently. "Oh, she's purring."

Maddy beamed. "She is! She must be feeling better, now she's home."

"Maddy!"

Maddy looked round, and saw Becky come racing across the playground. "How's Biscuit?"

"Loads better," Maddy said happily.

"She walking again now. She's got a bit of a limp, but it's not too bad."

"I bet you're fussing over her like anything." Becky laughed.

"I love spoiling her," Maddy admitted. She looked at Becky shyly. "Mum said I could ask you over, so you can see how she is."

Becky beamed. "Really? Yes, please! Can I come today? Just to pop in and see her on the way home?"

"Yes, of course." Maddy could feel her face going pink. She hadn't been sure if Becky would be as friendly at school as she had been over the weekend.

"Do you think Mrs Melling would let you move tables, now that Kate isn't here any more?" Becky asked thoughtfully. "There's space for you to sit with me and Lara and Keri."

"I suppose we could ask," Maddy said, going even pinker.

"Cool." Becky pulled her over to the little group of girls she'd been chatting to. "Have you got a photo of Biscuit in your bag to show everyone?"

"She looks different," Becky said thoughtfully, later on that afternoon as the girls sat in Maddy's kitchen, watching Biscuit sleeping in her basket.

"The scratches don't look as bad," Maddy suggested.

"No, it isn't that. I think she just looks happier. I suppose she must have been feeling really miserable on Saturday." She glanced at the door. "Did your dad get that special cat flap?"

"Yes. And then he went round and worked out the times Biscuit gets to go outside with Josh's dad. He told Dad he'd already rung the vet. Tiger and Tom are booked in for Wednesday. Once they're neutered, the vet said he was sure they'd be less fierce."

"That's amazing." Becky grinned. "Aren't you glad I made you go and ring their bell? Oh look, Biscuit's awake!"

Biscuit opened her eyes and yawned, showing her raspberry-pink tongue.

Then she looked lovingly at Maddy, and stepped out of her basket and on to Maddy's lap. She gave Becky a curious stare.

"Can I stroke her?"

Maddy nodded. "She doesn't seem as jumpy as she did before. It can't really be the new cat flap, because she hasn't even been out yet."

"Maybe she's just glad to be home," Becky suggested.

Maddy smiled down at Biscuit. She seemed to be going back to sleep again, just on a warmer, cosier sort of bed.

Biscuit burrowed deeper into Maddy's school cardigan, and purred softly with each breath. She was safe now. And she wasn't frightened any more.

HOLLY WEBB

Holly Webb started out as a children's
book editor and wrote her first series for
the publisher she worked for. She has been
writing ever since, with over one hundred
books to her name. Holly lives in Berkshire,
with her husband and three young sons.
Holly's pet cats are always nosying around
when she is trying to type on her laptop.

For more information
about Holly Webb visit:

www.holly-webb.com